Christopher's Story

A tale by Rick Arbour

ISBN-10: 1480076570
ISBN-13: 978-1480076570

DEDICATION

To my sons, without whom this book would not have been possible.
And to my wife, without whom my sons would not have been possible.

CONTENTS

1 SUDDEN DEPARTURE

Christopher sat on the rock for a very long time. No matter how many times he went through a time-door, it always made him dizzy. And this time, he had been separated from his father. He knew his father would find his way to wherever it was that Christopher had emerged eventually, but meanwhile he was on his own. "Where" was actually an easy thing to figure out. "When" would take guesswork, and probably a lot of tries.

It always helped him to think things through until the dizziness went away, so Christopher thought about the events that had led up to his sitting on this rock. When he last saw his father, they both stood in a small room lined with shelves of books. They had just completed a successful assignment protecting a prince on a long journey, and not everyone had been happy that they were successful. It was an unexpected act of revenge by a would-be king that had separated them. Both of them had to react instinctively, and momentarily trust that Christopher's path could be retraced later.

Christopher didn't want to think about what would have happened if he, *if they,* didn't get out in time. The time-doors that they had been programming opened up right where and when they should have, and they dove through. But being rushed meant that while he knew *where* he was, he didn't know *when.*

Before parting, Christopher had asked his father to set his time-door to take him to their vacation cottage. It lay in a simple little world where he could rest for a week or so until school began in the fall. His father, on the other hand, had to wrap up the paperwork on their assignment in their home world where there were a lot of rules, regulations, and technology. The doors were only partially programmed and still warming up when the "infernal machine" as his father would call a bomb, rolled in the room.

As Christopher's time-door opened, it glowed blue meaning that it was a place where magic still existed, and he preferred that. But you had to keep on your toes, because pretty much anything could happen. What's worse, the blast could have affected his passage and there was no telling what this world would turn out to be like.

As he sat, a small wagon pulled by an ox and driven by an old farmer and his wrinkled wife approached the crossroads from the south. They slowed as they saw him, but continued coming.

His head was clearer so he stood slowly, taking stock of his surroundings. He realized that he was familiar with the crossroads. The road leading west would bring him straight to the family cottage. He noticed that his dark green cape was smoking from the blast and he absent-mindedly dunked it in a nearby puddle of water to put it out while the farmer's wife watched out of the corner of her eye.

"Scat, Fred, I swear he weren't there a moment ago, and look how he's afire! Tsk, I shouldn't be surprised to see him sprout wings and take off next! Land sakes, what's this kingdom coming too, these days? This used to be a quiet neighborhood, but things shore have changed!" she hissed.

Christopher, whose hearing was pretty good (except for the ringing caused by the explosion) overheard this and wished that he really could sprout wings. Yes, he was close to home, but it would still be a good half a day before he could get there on foot and the sun was already high in the sky.

As the creaking ox cart slowly dwindled out of sight rocking back and forth up the north road, Christopher put his cape back over his shoulders, pulled the hood over his head to shade him from the late summer sun, and started walking westward, to the family cottage and a weeklong rest.

The rest of the afternoon was uneventful although he encountered a few travelers who were heading east. They gave him a wide berth, watching him suspiciously until they were out of sight behind him. One even waggled his first and last fingers at him in a magical sign designed to ward off evil while mumbling a brief incantation. This behavior rather surprised Christopher, since he was only a small boy, and the travelers were grown men. While he was surprisingly able to take care of himself in a scuffle, they had no way of knowing that. And at any rate, they seemed to be more concerned that he might put a spell on them rather than attack them physically. Normally, grown men are quite unafraid of small travelers. "This doesn't smell right." He thought to himself.

Still, he traveled on admiring the view of the mountain ranges to the west and to the north of the low plain he now walked through. As he went he entertained himself by humming tunes, and stopping from time to time to investigate a particularly interesting mud puddle or rock, and once to stuff a rather fine example of a ptarmigan feather into his back pack for his collection at the cottage.

The family cottage lay at the foot of the mountains so that the sun disappeared behind them well before sunset, but he was still able to get to the cottage before it grew dark. The cottage stood at the top of a hill, overlooking a fork where the road he now traveled would merge with one from the southeast. At the spot where the two roads met, the combined road continued on west by north-west eventually curving northwards until it was lost from sight in the shadows of the mountains.

As the fork came into view he thought he noticed some movement at the far side of the valley but it was getting a bit darker and the distance was still far enough that he wasn't sure. Walking further though, he made out two or three small figures moving towards him from the other road. As he neared the fork he lost sight of them briefly behind one of the foothills, and they never got as far as the fork. It made Christopher curious but not alarmed. After all, it was getting dark, and if they were travelers they would have to pick out a camp site before it grew too dark to find sufficient scrub brush and other dead wood around the hills that would provide them with firewood for the night.

At the fork, Christopher softly spoke the incantation that would make the cottage appear at the crest of the hill, and allow him to enter.

Trudging slowly up the hill, he turned to look back out over the plain and enjoy the view. Turning to the southeast, he could see the small orange glow of a campfire reflecting off a spire of lazily rising smoke in the fading twilight.

Entering the cottage, his eyes wandered around the room taking in the familiar objects, and he began to relax. He scanned the hearth where the pots hung on wooden hooks, the dining table where some of his fathers old books were stacked, the shelves where old pictures of his family sat side-by-side with keepsakes like feathers, rocks, and small leather pouches.

Looking up into the rafters, he saw two round eyes staring straight back at him, and said softly "Heart! You old rascal! Am I glad to see you! Been keeping the place free of mice, have you?" The barn owl whoooed softly in response, and glided down to the table where Christopher could stroke his head and neck. Before long though, he flew back up to his exit hole in the peak of the wall and soared off in search of a meal.

Christopher stepped over to the round window by the door, but it was too dark to see far now, and he spoke the magic words of protection which again hid the cottage from view.

He took the flint and steel from the shelf over the hearth and struck them together over a small pile of fluffy tinder. A spark caught and glowed in the fluff, and he blew gently until it became a bright smoking red star, stopping to watch as it burst into a tiny flame. He stuffed the tinder under the kindling that was already carefully stacked like a teepee in the fireplace and, settling down in one of the overstuffed chairs that sat to either side of the hearth, fumbled in his bag for a bite. "Good thing I brought some peanut butter sandwiches." He said to himself. "I'm too tired to cook and too hungry to wait!"

Christopher sat with his feet out in front of him eating the sandwich and drinking water from his canteen. He watched the small fire until he drifted off to sleep.

2 BREAKFAST GUESTS

The sun was already two hand spans from the horizon when Christopher awoke. The fire had long ago died, and all that was left was a cold pile of ash and charcoal. "Peanut butter sandwiches just aren't going to cut it this time." He said to himself. Looking up, he added "Hey Heart! Got any extra mice you want to share for breakfast? I'm starved!" Heart looked down over his shoulder from his perch on a rafter as if to say "You should have put in your order last night" and then, blinking his eyes slowly, stuffed his head under a wing.

"Oh well, I never did much care for mice anyway." Christopher said, and rummaged through the pack he'd brought for something appropriate. He found a banana and a rather flat jelly donut, and he filled a mug with fresh water from a squeaky water pump at the sink. The first meal or two at the cottage was always a bit simple, until the locals knew that they were back and more substantial fare became available. He mumbled to himself "Boy, I must be hungrier than I thought. I would swear I can smell fresh bread."

Deciding to eat out on the front steps where he could enjoy the view of the valley, he scooped up his meal and mug, walked to the door, stepped out, and immediately tripped over a gray bearded dwarf in a brown cape.

"Arrrghmmph!" Christopher yelped as he spilled his mug of water, tumbled forward face first into his jelly donut and then tumbled completely over onto his back. A second dwarf leapt over to him wide-eyed and, peeling the donut off Christopher's face, shouted "Smarstick! Ye've kilt 'im!"

"No, no, Smartwig, I think he's alive," the first dwarf said, "see how his eyes be rolling around? If he were dead, they'd be sorta jest pokin' out, without all that movin' about."

Christopher's eyes were indeed rolling around, because there were now not two, but three dwarves bent over him and he was watching each one momentarily before moving his eyes on to the next in a continuous circle. The two dwarves who had spoke thus far then reached down and, each grabbing an elbow, helped Christopher to sit up. "Step back and let the lad get his wits about him, you two!" spoke the third Dwarf. Are you hurt, son?"

"How, how..." Christopher stuttered "I mean, you can't... I didn't... the cottage! It's not there! I mean, it is there, but you couldn't know that!"

The dwarf's eyebrows raised momentarily, and then the look of concern on his face was replaced with relief.

"Ah, that. Well, yes. 'Tis true, it isn't to be seen with the eyes then, is it? But we've brought along a bit better fare than the one ye be wearing all over yer nose, and if ye'd be kind enough to break yer fast with us, I'd be happy to explain why we showed up so unexpectedly on yer door."

And although Christopher's first impulse was to decline the offer, smoke was already rising from the chimney because one of the dwarves had restarted fire and the smell of bacon was wafting out the door.

As the dwarf wiped the powdered sugar off Christopher's face, he said "Oh, forgive my manners, young man, of course ye'd be hesitant to share a meal with three men ye don't know, and all. I be Smarlog, leader of the Smar clan, and these two 'BUFFOONS!'" (he shouted past Christopher with a glare towards the cottage door) "be me brothers Smarstick and Smartwig. Ye'll have to forgive 'em if ye can, they mean well, and they meant ye no harm."

"Oh, sure." Christopher said although he still wasn't very sure at all. But being back on his feet helped him feel a bit more secure, especially since he now saw that he stood a head taller than Smarlog, who was the tallest of the three.

They entered the cottage, where Smartstick and Smartwig had quickly set the table which seemed hard pressed to keep from collapsing under the weight of the bacon, eggs, sausage, milk, fruit, juice, and breads piled high on it. "Where did all this food come from? I didn't see you carry all this in!" Christopher said.

"Well, we can't always set a table this well, but we met up with a local farmer late yesterday afternoon, and knowing we were near the home of the adventurer we seek, we bargained a bit. It may be the last fresh meal we see for a while." Smarlog said.

"Oh? Are you going somewhere where food is hard to find?" asked Christopher.

"Sit and enjoy, and we'll explain after." Smarlog replied in a way Christopher found rather secretive. Even though still unsure of the three, the sight and smell of the meal was just too tempting and he sat down to feast.

Once the meal had been consumed by the five diners (if you include Heart, who landed in Smartwigs plate briefly to claim a particularly juicy sausage and startling Smartwig so badly he fell backward off his bench) the remains were packed away into a small back pack. Looking at the pack, which didn't seem large enough to hold everything he saw go into it Christopher was reminded that Smarlog never really did answer his question about how they'd found the cottage. He became convinced that there was more than a little magic behind it all. "Are you wizards?" he asked them.

"No." Smarlog said, frowning. "Oh, we know the occasional spell, and some that are more useful for travelers, but we don't study the arts the way you mean. Our clan has always been more concerned with other matters than the control of magic. We be craftsmen, and tradesmen. Sometimes we will trade our crafts for useful magic, and in a way, that's what brought us here this morning."

Christopher felt this was a good start, but only a start, and pressed for more answers.

"Let me start at the beginning." Smarlog said. "Many years ago, when my grandfather was a lad, and his father was the clan leader, there was a sorcerer who lived at the very edge of our kingdom. He often needed things made, and since our clan is famous as craftsmen, it was no surprise that he'd call on us. Sorcerers can do much, but there's precious little magic that can work silver and gold or dig a mine or build a castle like a dwarf can, especially a dwarf of the Smar clan. And some of the things he needed made were peculiar, and had to be jes so."

"Peculiar? In what way?"

"Wal, amulets be amulets, be'ent they? And they often must mimic life. Some of them looked more like animals than animals do, and he gave directions so sure that these could move, sometimes on their own, even before they were completely crafted. That was near the end that he had us makin' those cursed things, and that was when we drew the line. But by then, it was jes too late."

Smartwig and Smarstick shook their heads in sorrow, agreeing with Smarlog. By now, the four had moved to the front steps again where this all began, and they sat looking out over the valley. Smarstick was drawing strange characters in the dirt, and smartwig appeared to be moving food from one pocket to another as if taking stock to be sure that he had enough.

Christopher didn't know what to ask next, but Smarlog was making an honest effort to complete the picture. "Oh, we got paid right well for the work we'd done 'im, all right. At first, it was gems and such, and gold. "But as his needs grew, and we grew used to him and his ways, he started suggestin' there were other ways ter be paid, and I guess he mebbe even had some control over me great-grandpa by then, and started payin' us in magic. Thet's why we knew where yer house was, and who ye be." He added helpfully.

Christopher's heart suddenly raced much faster. From the time he learned to talk, he had been told over and over again that 'when we are off in these other places we never, never, never tell them we are from another world'. "Who I be? I mean, who I am?" he stammered.

Smarlog looked at Smarstick and Smartwig, and nodded. As if by agreement, they both got up and started wandering the top of the hill around the house, as if on patrol. Smarlog lowered his voice, and looked Christopher straight in the eyes. "Yer naught from here, son, thet we know. We don't know from where, but here, it ain't. We've never seen magic quite the color o' yourn, and it was harder than bitin' the scales off a good sized dragon to find ye. No, yer not from here."

There was a moment of silence, while Christopher gathered his wits, and then slowly said the lines he'd rehearsed his whole life, in case of just such a situation. "Well we come from nearly the other side of the…"

"No, no, lad." Smarlog interrupted, waving a hand. "I don't blame ye a bit fer bein' guarded, but I'm talkin' as straight as I know how, te tell ye jest how serious this matter is. Ye see, there were other sorcerers back then too. And not all of them was as schemin' as this'n spoke of. It was they who foretold of a lad from another world thet would be the only chance we had o' reclaimin' our home. And one by one, they were done in by thet black-hearted ogre-lovin' son of a swamp…" Smarlog looked sheepish. "Sorry, I git a tad carried away when I think on it too much."

Christopher decided that the best way to avoid admitting he was not from this world was to change the subject, and since Smarlog was so fanatic about the sorcerer, it seemed the best subject to change to. "What did he do, once you refused to work for him?"

"Wal, now, it seems he'd been bidin' his time for years and years, jes settin' us up. We'd been buildin' him his castle, and He'd even suggested changes to ours that our clan leaders agreed to. At the time, they seemed to make sense. There warn't any real enemies this side o' the great ocean, and at any rate, the walls and sech he suggested seemed as solid as they come. No army coulda done 'em in."

Smarlog laughed without humor. "No army." He said as he looked up into the sky.

Suddenly, Christopher caught on to what he meant. "An air force?" he blurted out before he realized that there was no such thing in this world. Airplanes were centuries away.

"Air force? Wal, I ain't never heard of a dragon called an air force before, but it ain't sech a bad term, is it?" Smarlog said.

8

Christopher's neck hurt from the force as his head spun around to Smarlog. "Yow! Did you say dragon? Smarlog, there's a lot of magic in this world, but dragons? That's over the edge! They're mythical!"

Smarlog's head was now hanging down. "Wal, thet used ter be true, sure enough. Until we built 'im one." He said softly.

3 A BUMPY START

Once the whole story had come out, there wasn't much Christopher could have done that would have changed what happened next. Smarlog's ancestors had lost their lands to the black Sorcerer by trickery, deceit, magic, and in the end by murder and theft as well. He'd tricked them into making his dragon piece by piece, performing the final assembly himself in the confines of his own castle and even had them building him an army of ogres in the same way until they realized what they were and refused to build more. But by that time he had completed the dragon and used it to attack the dwarves' castle, killing many dwarves, enslaving the best craftsmen, and driving the rest into exile.

Christopher now found himself preparing to go on a journey without the help or even the knowledge of his father, to help three dwarves that he'd just met save their kingdom from a black Sorcerer and a dragon based on the prophecy of someone who'd died long before his father was born. And yet, searching his heart, he couldn't see how he could do anything else even if he also couldn't see what one small boy could do to tip the scales.

Looking around the cottage, he took his old backpack and stuffed it with the things he imagined he'd need most. Rope, a sturdy knife, a compass, a bedroll, a canteen and a dozen peanut butter sandwiches (which he was now very thankful he'd thought to pack yesterday before he had any inkling of what his vacation would turn into.) "They may look pretty tired by the time I get to finish the last one, but they may make a difference too." He thought to himself.

He strapped a short sword around his waist, and took up an oak walking stick with a falcon's head carved on the knob. Then, as an afterthought, he dug around in a small chest in the corner of the cottage, and found a small leather bag with eight marbles in it which he stuffed into his pack. The marbles looked harmless enough, but he smiled thinking of times past when

10

he'd been forced to use them, and what powerful, if unpredictable, magic they contained.

Next he sat down at the table and carefully wrote a note to his father, explaining that he had been recruited to help straighten out a problem with someone's property, and the general direction they would be going. He left out that the problem included chasing out a dragon. He thought that his father might worry a bit over that.

Finally he was ready, and stepped out of the cottage. Turning to take one last look before casting the spell, he saw Heart's face in the round window next to the front door. "You keep those mice out of our flour, now, Heart. It's up to you to watch the place until I get back." Then he whispered the words that hid the cottage, and Heart's face faded from view.

Christopher now found that he was nervous about this trip, and wishing he had come into a world that was just a little bit less magical. There was no question that this was going to be a dangerous and difficult task, and they had very far to go. The four struck off north-west up the road that curved to the northern mountains. None of them noticed when Heart, who should have been fast asleep by this time resting for his evening hunt, glided out the hole in the peak of the cottage wall, and quietly soared into the sky over the foothills to the south.

The day was warm and dry, and the road dusty. By late afternoon, they were as far from the cottage as Christopher had ever wandered and he found himself studying his surroundings to learn more about the area.

The mountains to the north seemed just as far off as they were when they took the road curving toward them this morning, and Christopher could see that it would be days before they got to their foothills. On the left now were cultivated fields as far as the eye could see. Rolling plains of even rows of carrots waved in the light summer breeze, giving it the appearance of a dark green sea. Smarlog did not know much about this land, except to say that they called the man who controlled it the Carrot Baron, and that the field workers that he'd met walking this road (which bordered the carrot baron's property) were not very talkative, except about carrots. "They'll talk yer ear off about the different kinds. Which are sweeter, and which are better fer stews, and which have bigger cores and all. It were enough to make my head spin. I never knew there were so much to know about 'em. But talk te them about anythin' else - tools, crafts, travel - they jest shrug their shoulders, an' ask what it's got ter do with carrots."

"And don't go pickin' a carrot, either," he added "'cause they watch these fields like hawks and if ye so much as pluck a green, ye'll have fifteen angry carrot farmers down on ye faster'n ye kin say 'orange root'!" He added.

Smartwig nodded in agreement. "I made that mistake once, and I still have the bump on my head te prove it!" he said, pulling back his hood and pointing to a spot on his head.

Smarstick added "An' that's sayin' a mouthful, cause there be'ent much what kin keep between Smartwig and a meal!" The three dwarves chuckled at that, and Christopher realized that Smartwig had been eating one thing or another, pretty much since they'd set off that morning.

"What about the other side of the road?" Christopher asked. "What's behind this hedge?"

"Wal, now, behind this hedge is grasslands, with an awful odd lot of characters wanderin' them. I been told that they grew this hedge te keep 'em outta the carrot fields. Seems they're kinda soft on 'em, and they're too fast fer the farmers te catch. Fer all that, they seem a harmless lot. Naught but runnin' seems ter concern 'em. Cain't see what else they could do fer mischief." They acts a bit crazy more often than not, makin' noises like horses and runnin' across the plain like mad, in big bunches.

"Like a herd?" Christopher asked.

"Heard what?" Smarlog responded.

"No, not heard, herd. Like a horse herd." Christopher explained.

"Wal what do I care what a horse heard?" asked Smarlog.

"Never mind," replied a frustrated Christopher, "it wasn't important." But he thought Smarlog was hiding a smile behind his hand as he rubbed his nose.

The weather continued to be dry, and that night they camped under a huge old oak tree planted by the carrot farmers for noon-day shade. There was not enough wood around for a campfire, however, so the four dined on Christopher's aging peanut butter sandwiches.

He also noticed that Smartwig finished an extra half of one offered him by Smarlog, and when Christopher offered him yet another, he stuffed it in his pocket 'Fer later'. Even at that, you could see him staring sadly at the vast fields of untouchable carrots.

In the morning as they started off, Christopher was worried that the walking would become tedious and boring. But within an hour, the scenery began to change and the carrot fields were replaced by a rough scrub land with brambles and various dry looking weeds. By noon, the hedge curved steadily off away from them, and the road aimed directly north towards the distant mountains. The grasslands were replaced by an old forest, where huge old hardwood trees shadowed laurels and other thick growth, and the land was hillier than the fields and plains had been.

As they progressed, the brambles to the left and the growth to the right encroached closer and closer to the road, until you could almost grab handfuls of leaves on the right or thorns on the left without leaving the road.

Smartwig and Smarlog were walking alongside each other with

Christopher and Smarstick behind them when suddenly, six armed men blocked the road in front of them. A noise from behind made the four travelers turn about to see six more men close behind them.

"Give up yer valuables and ye'll naught be hurt." Said one of the men in front. Christopher thought he looked rather more nervous than he would have expected of a bandit, especially when they outnumbered their prey by three to one. Smarlog however, was not used to being told what to do and at any rate his pack contained equipment he desperately needed when he arrived at his destination and he was not about to give it up without a fight.

Since the four travelers were wearing their capes over their shoulders, it also apparently had escaped the bandit's notice that they were armed. So it came as a complete surprise when Smarlog drew a short sword from under his cloak and smacked the bandit who had spoken, with the flat side of his blade, knocking him to the ground senseless. At nearly the same moment, a buzzing like an angry hornet erupted from the vicinity of Smarstick, who had unleashed a slingshot and caught one of the bandits in the forehead. Smartwig wasted no time in kicking a third in the shins, and by that time Smarstick had reloaded and another bandit fell. Christopher swung his heavy walking stick around behind him at ankle height which had the effect of sweeping the feet out from under all six men standing behind him, and the remaining two bandits yet to be dealt a blow immediately threw their arms to the ground, and shouted "Stop! Stop! We give up!"

"Ye be the sorriest lot of robbers I ever laid eyes on!" Smarlog snarled. "I suggest ye find yerselves another line o' work, cause it's plain as the nose on my face that ye'll starve in this one!"

Sitting in the road and rubbing the rising bump on his head where Smarlog had struck him, the spokesman for the robbers said "Well, to be honest, that's because we be'ent robbers at all, and if we coulda kept feedin' our families by farmin', we'd have never tried this. But, that cursed black cloud has been the death of our farms. And it's been years since any good amount of travelers have been on this road, an', well, we were desperate, and ye looked well fed, and we figgered ye could spare a loaf o' bread without too much pain."

It was indeed plain that these 12 men had seen better times, and there wasn't one among them that couldn't have used a few extra pounds. Smarlog frowned, but Christopher recognized this as one of concern, not of anger.

"Wal, what do we do with yer now?" He complained. "It's plain we don't want yer wanderin' where ye can cause more mischief, and there's naught much fer law in these parts where we can bring ye fer judgement. But what foolishness made yer turn to robbery? And what's this black cloud ye spoke of?"

"These hills of thorns and briars ye be walking in were once all farmlands, where we grazed our sheep and goats." explained another of the robbers. "But for years, every few days, a black cloud spills out over the land from the mountains to the west, and it has done terrible things. With less sun our grazing lands grew poorer and when it rains, the black soot it leaves behind make our crops and livestock ill, not to mention us. Most everybody's moved on, but we twelve stuck it out, hopin' against hope that someday the cloud would stop or we'd figger out what were causin' it and stop it."

Smarstick looked at Smarlog. "It's him, ain't it!" he said.

"Wal, we don't know fer sure, but I would bet that it is." Smarlog said.

"Him who?" said the twelve robbers in unison as if they were a singing group.

Smarlog gave the twelve a brief account of the rise of the black sorcerer. They began to ask, then demand that Smarlog allow them to come along, so they could help. Smarlog was not keen on the idea. "What, so ye kin rob us in the dead o' night and run off?" But they were insistent and sincere, and even went so far as to threaten to follow the four anyway, and that they may as well go together. "There's strength in numbers." One pointed out. "And we'd be willin' te carry any extra gear ye pick up fer the job." offered another.

Finally, Smarlog agreed to allow them to accompany the small band "But the first sign o' monkey business and ye'll get worse than the flat o' this sword!" he threatened.

"Wal, if we're to be travelin' with ye, we'd best be knowin' yer names." Smarlog said. "Somebody speak up."

Again, all twelve men spoke at once. "George."

"Not all at once, fer heavens sake! And which one is George? Raise yer hand." Smarlog growled.

Obediently, all twelve of the farmer bandits raised their hand.

"No no, only the one named George, ye bunch a sod bustin' knuckleheads!" Smarlog shouted.

"But we're all named George!" said one of the men.

"What? Oh boy!" Said Christopher. "We can't call them all George, this is too confusing!"

Suddenly Smartwig grinned, and said "I got it! Everybody line up!"

Obediently, the twelve men got in a line in front of the little dwarf.

Smartwig walked down the line, reaching up and poking each in the stomach as he said "One, Two, Three, Four, Five, Six, Seven, Eight, Nine, Ten, Eleven, Twelve. Now, everybody remember yer numbers!"

Smarstick looked at Smarlog with a smirk and said "Wal, it's simple but effective, ain't it?"

4 RAIDERS!

The expanded band now struck back off down the road as night began to fall. The farmers told them of an old inn just up the road, but warned them that this late in the day it was unlikely that they would be allowed in.

"They lock up like a little fort, once the sun goes down. It's safer fer them that get there in time, what with all the bad eggs that've taken to this road of late."

The inn turned out to be a crude but well built two story affair. Made from logs, and with small heavily shuttered windows, it appeared quite able to withstand an attack.

The others stayed by the road while Christopher went forward alone to bang on the door, after which a small peep-hole opened in the door over his head.

"Who's out there?" said a voice.

"We're weary travelers, looking for a warm hearth and a hot meal." said Christopher.

"I can't see you! Do you think I'm going to let invisible travelers into my inn? Why I'd never know where you were!" said the voice.

"I'm not invisible, I'm just short!" said Christopher, stepping back from the door so the innkeeper could see him.

"A dwarf, eh? Tsk tsk. I should think not. Strange rascals now, aren't you? How many of you are there?" said the voice.

"No, I'm not a dwarf, I'm just a boy, although there are three dwarves in our party." Christopher said. "And twelve farmers."

"No, I'm afraid that you'll have to move on, sir. We have a policy, you know. This late in the day, one never knows what could be knockin' on the door. And one, and three, and twelve, why that's uh, um, oh, twenty-five or so. No, we couldn't possibly…."

"Twenty-five! There are only sixteen of us!" Christopher corrected him.

"Mind your manners lad!" said the innkeeper hotly. "At any rate, I'm in here, where I'm staying, and you're out there, where you're staying! These days, it's better to be safe than sorry, and we're not opening the door to a pack of dwarves this late at night!"

With that, the small peep-hole slammed shut, and Christopher walked slowly back to the road where the travelers waited.

"They won't let us in." Christopher announced to the troupe.

"Perhaps if Smarlog speaks to them." Suggested Smarstick.

"I'm afraid he's not terribly fond of dwarves." Christopher replied, rather embarrassed. "I'm sorry. I don't know why, exactly."

"No need to apologize, lad, we hear that more often than not when we're on the road. People be scared o' what they don't know." Smarlog said. "And it's gettin' way past when we ought ter be settlin' down. We'd best find us an out of the way spot back in the forest, where we aren't a target fer them what travels this road after dark te hide their doin's."

Number One told them of a spot not far where they'd camped previously, but warned that going into the forest might be as dangerous as not. "There be creatures aplenty a wanderin' around in there, and we was up all night in shifts, keepin' a sharp eye out."

But seeing no alternative, the group followed Number One along the side of a stream into the darkening woods, collecting kindling for a small fire on the way. Soon they had passed over a few hills, and were out of sight of the road. Coming upon a small flat area halfway up a hill and overlooking a stream, Number One announced they had arrived at their destination. "Pull up a stump while we git the fire lit." he added. "It ain't much, but it beats sleepin' in the ruts of the road."

Smarlog looked around doubtfully. "We've got precious little warning if we're attacked here, what with all the underbrush. And lightin' a fire half-way up the hill like this could attract every ne'er-do-well this side of the mountains."

Still, with the onset of darkness, there was little to do but make the best of it. So they dug a pit to make spotting the fire harder, and after sharing a small meal, sent Number Five, Number Six, Number Seven, and Number Eight out into the brush a bit to act as sentries. "We'll replace ye by the numbers in two hours. Numbers Nine through Twelve next, then us Dwarves and Christopher, Then One through Four." Smarlog ordered.

Christopher dozed fitfully, until Smartwig woke him sometime after midnight.

"It's our spell." Smartwig whispered.

Noticing Smarlog was taking his pack with him, Christopher motioned to it and gave Smarlog a questioning look.

"Too much magical in here to trust with anyone but meself, I'm afraid. As much as I'd like to think it'll be fine here, I'm responsible fer me clan, and their last hope lies in you and in this pack." He said.

For the next hour, Christopher sat huddled on a rock, watching down over the stream at the foot of the hill and wondering about Smarlog's comment. It was the darkest part of the night, and the sliver of moon that had at least shed the thinnest of light into the forest where the trees didn't block it out had long since set. Even so, his eyes had adjusted to the dark to the point where he could see motion at the corner of his vision, and three, and then four times, he was sure something moved under the laurels. Once he thought he heard the rustle of leaves.

"It's likely just a rabbit or something looking for a meal" he thought to himself. His attention had begun to drift somewhat when a tiny pebble hit him on the back. It seemed to come from the direction of Smartwig's post.

Christopher felt sure it was Smartwig warning him that something was moving near him as well, and to stay alert.

Sure enough, there was a sudden rush of several dark bodies in the bushes by Christopher, but too far away for him to intercept as they ran past. With a shout to warn the others, he chased after them. They sounded light-footed, and only the lower brush seemed to shake as they pushed through it. Christopher couldn't be sure what they were. They ran straight into the encampment where they seemed to be intent on causing confusion.

By now, shouting was coming from all the lookouts, and the twelve farmers were flailing about with whatever was at hand. Two were rolling around the now dark fire, wrestling with the assailants. Christopher threw some fresh kindling on the fire to light the scene, but ran back out into the brush when he heard Smarlog shouting in anguish. "Me pack! Me pack! Give me that back, ye son of a divil!"

And with that, the fire flared into life, illuminating the farmers and dwarves, swinging and wrestling madly with what appeared to be at least two dozen wolves.

But with Smarlog's shout, and a brief "yip" from one of the wolves, the attack was over as fast as it had begun. Those wolves wrestling on the ground were aided by the others who had not been involved with direct attacks on the travelers, and they faded into the undergrowth like so many shadows. For a few seconds, they could hear the rustling of leaves as the attackers fled, but even that faded quickly into silence.

Smarlog was beside himself with anger. "They seemed to be intent on stealin' me pack!" he shouted. "I nivir had a chance! The Divils overcame me by numbers before I could raise me sword, grabbed me pack, and were done with me!"

The group took assessment. Of all the packs, the only ones taken were two carried by the dwarves, and Christopher's. The one dwarf pack left behind, was the one with the remaining food.

"But why would hungry wolves take everything but the food?" asked Number One.

The three dwarves looked at each other with concern. "They know too much, if ye ask me." Smarlog growled. "There be only one reason I kin think of to take jest those packs, and it's got to do with thet black-hearted sorcerer! We've got to get those packs back, lads, or all is lost." Smarlog said.

"Surely we can find more supplies to replace them?" asked Number One.

"Mostly, yes." Smarlog replied, "But there's a secret or two in those packs that cannot be replaced, and hold the only hope we've got of succeedin'. We can't go on without those packs!" he said, the sorrow clear on his face. "We're doomed."

"Not so quick, we ain't!" said Number One. "Farmers we may be, but in these here parts, thet means bein' able to track game too, and there ain't one of the twelve of us what couldn't foller them cursed beasts right to their dens. Soon as it get's light, we're after 'em, boys." He said, as he turned to his eleven compatriots. Grimly, they nodded back.

Light was slow in coming, or at least it felt that way. The group gathered up everything they had meanwhile, and repacked it carefully, to make no noise. "We don't want 'em spookin' before we git close enough to say 'howdy'." Number Twelve explained to Christopher.

Privately, Christopher wondered what sort of 'howdy' the sixteen of them were going to be able to give to the wolf-pack, but he was sure that with the look of steel in the eyes of the men and the dwarves, there were going to be some sparks.

All that day, and into the next, the band followed the trail. For hours, Christopher had to take their word that they were indeed following any trail at all. But an occasional hair stuck on a low branch, or a few scuffed leaves seemed to be enough to the farmers.

Finally, in the afternoon, the trail happened to cross a muddy stream, and they could see actual footprints. The prints were huge, as wide as Christopher's boot. Studying the tracks for some time, Number One told the dwarves, "They're walkin' single file, so it's hard to say fer sure, but there's at least two dozen, mebbe as many as thirty. We've nivir seen anythin' like it. These wolves have been headin' in pretty much the same direction all day long. Wolves usually have a territory, and they kinder patrol the edges, but they must've left their territory hours ago.

When the tracks broke into two groups, with half a dozen moving east, and the rest continuing north, Number One added to their knowledge again. "They don't know we're follerin' 'em. Or at least they don't act like it.

They're movin' slow and careful, not like they're bein' follered. But we're down to two dozen, ahead of us, if'n the six don't come back.

"How do we know the six don't have the packs?" Smarlog asked.

"A wolf ain't built te carry a backpack, and there's sure sign thet the ones we're a follerin' are still draggin' em along. Don't worry, they're there all right."

"I hope yer right, Number One." Smarlog said. "I trust ye, even though the way we met weren't so easy-goin'. But I can see in yer eyes, ye want us to succeed as bad as we do."

Number One looked sad. "We nivir woulda' done what we did if our family's weren't in sech need, and even at that, it weren't right. We nivir did apologize rightly, and I'm hopin' we kin make it up to ye."

Finally, the group found themselves at the base of those mountains that they'd gazed at from the carrot fields, days ago. They seemed to rise suddenly out of the forest like a castle. And the trail of the wolves led straight into a crevice in the mountainside. The crevice, a crack that ran up the cliff out of sight in the treetops, was wide enough for three men at a time. Number Two followed the tracks into the crevice, followed by the other farmers, then the dwarves. Christopher brought up the rear, but he had a strange feeling he wasn't the last one in line.

5 A SHAKY TRUCE

Christopher followed the band quietly along the sandy floor of the crevice. He could still see a slash of light over his head, which illuminated the passageway. The crack that they now walked through apparently split the mountain from its roots to its peak. The crevice was not straight though. The two sides split away from each other unevenly, and the band swung left and right over and over again, in a snaking motion. Christopher, aware that the sandy floor would prevent his hearing any approaching danger, was hard pressed to keep up with the excited group of men and dwarves, while keeping a safe eye behind them. Finally, worried that he would never be able to defend himself if a surprise attack developed, he stuck his walking stick with the falcon's head into a small crack in the side of the crevice wall. Then he murmured a brief spell he'd been taught to awaken the falcon head, and whispered "Tell me if we're followed."

The falcon head suddenly blinked, and then nodded.

Christopher ran on to catch up with the band of travelers. Just as he caught back up, he heard the shrill whistle of the falcon, and knew that his fears were founded. They were being followed, and not more that 30 or 40 feet behind. The falcon's call alerted the rest of the band as well, although they did not know where it came from, and they immediately turned and prepared for what might come. Moments later the wolves bounded around the corner (for it was the wolves of course, who had followed them into the crevice). But the wolves, realizing that they had been discovered, had expected that the band would panic and continue into the crevice, and the wolves could safely overpower them from behind. Instead, when they rounded the corner, they found themselves beset by the first four in line, including Christopher. And this time, without room to maneuver, the band of travelers had an advantage, and not only fought the wolves to a standstill, but in a flash of inspiration, Christopher had grappled with the lead wolf and shouted for some of the others to help him subdue it. This they did, while four more of the men leapt over them to continue to stand off the wolves. This completely confounded the remaining wolves, who seemed very concerned over the capture of one of their ranks.

Suddenly in a growling but lisping voice, one of the wolves distinctly said "Hurt him and none will leave this mountain! Let him go now!"

"They speak!" said Number Six, who happened to be one of the four defenders in the first row.

"Speak we do." Growled the wolf, "And mean what we say." He added.

Christopher, who had caught his breath by now, said over the shoulder of the men in front of him "The captive is safe enough. But we aren't about to let him go as easy as all that. We have something of yours. You have something of ours."

While the meaning of that sank in to the wolves, Smarlog worked his way up to stand next to Christopher. The captured wolf could not speak, since they were forced to tie his mouth shut for fear of being bitten. His legs were also all tied together underneath him. It looked quite uncomfortable, but couldn't be helped.

"He's got ter be important, or they would jest have kept comin'" Smarlog whispered to Christopher. "I think we got us a good bargaining chip, thanks to you!"

Christopher nodded. "A lucky break." He whispered back.

Now the wolf who had spoken stepped forward menacingly, causing the first row of men to lower their sword and spear points threateningly. "Trade? So you can poison our pups? I think we'd all rather die in battle here and now, human!" he growled.

"Poison your pups? What on earth are you talking about?" Christopher asked. "That's ridiculous. Why would we do such a thing?"

"The ways of men make no sense to us, human. How would we know why you do the things you do? We've been told you pack poisons into the forest that could kill our kin, and we'll not hand them over so easy."

"Told? By who?" Smarlog said. "I've not a thing in my pack that could harm a pup, yet you flea-bitten, oversized rodents have stolen the only thing that can save my clan, and I'll have it back!"

Christopher added, hoping Smarlog's angry insults would be forgotten "Yes, tell us, who told you we carry poison?"

"Not that it matters, but we call him 'The Old Man of the Forest'. What do you mean the only thing that can save your clan?" The wolf lisped. Smarlog's insult appears to have had less impact on him than his heated statement that his clan was in danger of being wiped out.

Smarlog, who had regained control of his temper now, said in a more level tone "What is in the bag is of no use or harm to a wolf pack, but could make the difference between dwarves bein' and not bein'. We've a deadly enemy ahead of us, and our packs carry magic meant fer him."

"Who is this old man you speak of?" Christopher asked the wolf. "Where is he? I think we need an explanation from him, especially if he lied to you about why we're here. Why, we were only in the forest for the night, we'd have been gone the next day." Turning to Smarlog, he added "He may be in leagues with the Sorcerer. I think we should find out what he's up to."

As much as Smarlog did not want to do anything that would sway them from their mission, he agreed that "If'n this old man is plottin' with the black-heart, we'd best not let him work behind us." Turning to the wolf, he said "Here's the deal, take it or leave it. We keep yer friend here til ye've led us to the old man. When we git there, we find out what this old man is about, and why he's spreadin' rumors like this about us, and we give ye yer friend, and ye give us our packs. And with naught missin', or sure as I stand here, some she-wolves'll be mournin' their missin' mates."

Christopher groaned inwardly. If the wolves didn't tear them apart after words like that, it would be a miracle.

But to his surprise, the wolves did agree to show the band the way to the old man, although they also warned Smarlog in return that if the captive wolf lost more than a few dozen hairs from the ordeal, there would be some well-fed pups by evening time.

The wolves backed away, and melted out of sight back down the passageway. It took four of the farmers to carry the captive wolf back. After the warning words of the wolf, they were quite ginger about it too. Christopher retrieved his walking stick from the crack in the wall as they returned. Smarlog watched Christopher whisper a few words over the falcon's head. The 'bird' blinked once again, and returned to its wooden state.

"Looks like we all got a few tricks up our sleeves." He said smiling.

"How did you know the wolves would go for such a tough bargain?" Christopher asked.

"I didn't" Smarlog replied. "It was clear we had someone important bound up, but I think they only agreed because they felt they'd been had by the old man too, and need to get to the bottom of this as much as we do."

"I think they know as much about being an endangered species as a dwarf." Christopher said thoughtfully.

Smarlog studied Christopher for a moment. "Aye, they do, lad. Mebbe we're more like them than I realized."

The band camped at the foot of the cliff that night, since the events of the day had taken much of the remaining daylight, and both parties had much to talk over. For some reason, Smarstick took charge of watching the wolf. They made an odd pair, the huge gray canine and the little dwarf. Smarstick checked the wolf's bindings, making sure they were secure, but comfortable. Then he fashioned a collar, and bound the wolf to a small tree at the campsite not too close to the fire. He even unbound the beast's muzzle and shared some of his dwindling food supply with him, after the wolf swore that he wouldn't try to escape.

Christopher decided to explore along the base of the cliff, and told Smarlog where he was heading.

"Don't ye think ye should take someone along, jest in case?" Smarlog suggested. But with the attack from the night before fresh in their minds, all of the men seemed occupied setting up a good defensive camp.

"Seems like closing the barn door after the horse is gone, if you ask me." Christopher said.

The men looked at each other sheepishly, and Number One said "Thet about sums it up, all right. But, still, better safe than sorry. Mebbe them wolves got plans they ain't sharin'."

"With a hostage, we're safe enough I think. They would gain little from waiting. Look at them, they're amongst us in the camp as we speak." Christopher replied, and as if to prove the point, one of the wolves strode up to where they stood. "If we're attacked tonight, it will be from a new enemy, I bet."

As Christopher started off, the wolf followed him at a distance. "If you are going to follow me, you might as well do it where we can talk." Christopher suggested. The wolf considered this, then trotted up along side of him. "I'm just going to see what there is to see, but I suspect you want to make sure I'm not causing any mischief, eh?"

"We made the mistake of underestimating you once. We didn't think you could or would track us so deep into the forest. Now that you're in the heart of our homeland, we'd be fools not to keep you in sight until we know what you're up to." He said.

Christopher shrugged. "Suit yourself."

Truth to tell, there was not much to see. The woods were old, and thick, and you couldn't see more than sixty or seventy feet before branches and tree trunks blocked your view, and there was relatively little wildlife about, at least that Christopher could see. So he kept the cliff in sight on his left, as the only landmark that he could use to find his way back to the camp.

As he rounded a curve in the cliff, he came across an overhang, where the cliff wall was protected from the elements. Walking under this jutting rock, Christopher noticed carvings on the wall, of what appeared to be a mastodon, and then one of a saber-toothed tiger chasing a man. The carvings were obviously old, largely worn away, even with the protection the overhang afforded. And yet, the man in the picture seemed somehow familiar.

"Who carved these?" Christopher asked.

The wolf sat, and gave a semblance of a shrug. "They've been there since before there was a forest." He said. "No one knows."

On impulse, Christopher stepped over to the right of the carvings, and using the hilt of his short sword, chipped a crude semblance of a falcon head into the cliff while the wolf watched quietly.

As he worked, Christopher said "Tell me about this old man. Is he evil?"

The wolf looked thoughtful for a moment. "Evil is not a word a wolf knows well. We learned it when we learned your speech. But as I understand it, I would say no. The Old Man of the Forest is neither evil nor good. He just, well, he just is."

Finishing the falcon head, Christopher said, "I guess we better get back. It's getting dark."

As they entered the campsite, Christopher could see that the men were upset. They had set their bedrolls close to the fire, and they started nervously as Christopher and the wolf came into sight. All were huddled as close as they could get to the fire, even though it was not a particularly cold night. Except, that is, the captive wolf (who was not fond of sparks on fur) and Smarstick, who seemed content enough to sit and talk with his newfound friend.

"Is there a problem? You all look kind of worried." Christopher said.

"Problem? I dare say there may be a big problem." Smarlog replied. By our reckoning, the sun ain't due te set fer another three or four hours, an' it be pitch dark out."

"It's the cloud!" Number One said. "The cloud is back! And that means trouble aplenty fer all, I fear."

They all fell silent. For a moment, all that could be heard was the crackling of the fire. Then they heard a sound like a brief rushing of wind, which faded and then resumed, faded and resumed, over and over again. The sound first seemed to be coming from the west. Gradually it moved, fading off to the east.

"Watchmen, keep extra sharp eyes out tonight, by thunder!" Number One said.

No one complained when the fire died down. Everyone hoped that the darkness would help keep them obscure.

6 DANGER IN THE DARK

Following Smartwig's example of the night before, a pile of pebbles was collected for each corner lookout that night. With any luck, they could communicate warnings of any pending attack to each other that much quicker without giving away their positions. The men and dwarves not on guard now moved up against the trees as well, to use as protection in case they were surprised in spite of their precautions. All that is, except Smarstick who, after sharing his dinner with the captive wolf, settled down to sleep next to him as well. The wolf was again muzzled, at the insistence of Smarlog. "Beggin' yer pardon, but we don't know ye well enough to trust ye won't chew through yer bonds and be off, and we've too much at stake ter take the chance."

The wolf nodded in understanding.

It was again after midnight that Christopher was awakened, but instead of the light touch of a dwarf, it was with a pebble in the head. He was as nervous as the others and never did drift into a deep sleep so it did not surprise him and he knew instantly what it must mean. Reaching out, he tapped the still form of Number Eleven, who was next to him. Number Eleven tapped back letting him know he was awake, and tapped the form next to him. Soon, in a human telegraph, all the men in the party were awake, lying still but waiting to see what happened next.

This time the noises were not as quiet or well placed. This time, whatever was approaching the camp did not appear to care if they knew it was coming. Number Eleven sat forward and put his lips close to Smarlog's ear. "By the sounds, it's on two legs, and very heavy." He whispered lightly.

Christopher heard the snick of Smarlog's sword leaving its sheath, and he did the same.

Suddenly, the slow steady tramping picked up its pace, as if running right at the camp. Real fear began to grip the group, for the approaching

25

attacker was so hefty, it actually shook trees as it ran. Smarstick quickly tossed a prepared mix of dry grass, leaves, and small sticks on the coals to the campfire, bringing it to life just as the attacker reached the outer ring of the site. The firelight momentarily distracted the huge form that now appeared. For a second, there was complete silence on both sides, as the men and Christopher gazed on the first ogre they had ever seen.

Then there was a tumult the like of which those woods had never seen. The ogre stood so tall, the tallest of the farmers came only to his waist. And he swung a club the size of a quarter of a cow, with mean iron spikes jutting from its knobbed end. Number Three, the target of the swing, was just able to jump back. He parried the blow with his spear, but the weight of the club alone was enough to thwart his block, and the huge rippling muscles of the ogre made it impossible for one man to stop.

But there were more than one man, and with a battle call that also shook the leaves, the twelve men now leapt in at the ogre from all sides, trying to get inside of the Ogre's murderous swing. For all his strength, he lacked the speed that the men had, and they were able to slow his advance into the camp. The wolf pack added their numbers to the fray when they could do so without interfering with the sword strokes of the men. But even so, the ogre continued moving slowly towards the center of the site, which was occupied by a wolf that was incapable of defending himself, and a dwarf who was unwilling to leave him.

While Smarstick stood his ground, carefully sorting through a pouch of rocks he held in his hand, much as a boy might when picking out his best marble, the rest of the band fought like demons. But they were tiring. Even though they were able to score hits and the ogre was bleeding profusely from several gashes in his legs, arms, and torso, he continued to move forward until he was within striking distance of the captive wolf. The tiny form of Smarstick was now the last line of defense left standing between the ogre and the wolf. The ogre raised his weapon high over his head with both hands, to crush the dwarf and wolf in one blow. So high did he lift the club, that the spikes were temporarily lost in the shadows of the leaves above.

Christopher felt like the scene now was playing out in slow motion. He leapt in from the ogre's right with a hacking action of his sword against the ogre's knee and although the blade bit in, it did little apparent damage. As his sword rebounded from the stroke, he could see that Smarstick was aiming his slingshot up at the ogre's head. He saw the perfectly round shiny stone as it rocketed from Smarstick's hand, and heard the now familiar buzz of the angry missile.

Smarstick had never pulled so hard on his slingshot, and his aim was never better. The rock, bigger than the others Christopher had seen him shoot before, made a resounding 'THWOCK' that echoed through the dark woods. Had this rock hit an ox in this way, his owner would have been sharpening his butcher knife afterward, for surely it would have caved in his skull. The ogre dropped his club and staggered backward two huge steps from the impact, and there was a rushing noise in the brush around the ogre as two dozen wolves all leapt upon him at once. The weight pushed him further off balance, and he fell backwards to the ground with a crash.

Smarstick had wasted no time in watching the results of his defense. When he saw that the immediate danger was at least detained he turned to the wolf and, drawing a small dagger, cut the muzzle, bonds, and collar off of the wolf. "It's plain it be you he's come fer, and I'll not let ye die like a trussed up chicken."

The captive wolf now dashed into the rolling body of fur and ogre at the edge of the light. Unbelievably, the ogre struggled to his feet, and seeing that his prey was now loose, he turned and loped off into the woods, with the wolf pack at his heels.

The men now stood gasping for breath, leaning on their swords and spears. Smarlog watched as the now freed wolf ran after the ogre and observed "It's plain he was here fer one reason, and one reason only." Turning to Smarstick, he added "Well, ye've loosed the one bargaining chip we had to git our bags back. I hope ye know what yer doin'."

"He'll be back." Smarstick said, looking his brother in the eye. "He gave his word."

Christopher thought Smarlog showed just why he was the leader of the Smar clan, when he replied "I trust ye little brother. Now let's bind our wounds and pick up this mess while we wait fer 'em to git tired o' chasin' thet thing around the woods and come back." So the wounded sat on a fallen log, and let the others wrap bandages over their various cuts scrapes and bruises.

"Not a broken bone among us!" Number One observed as Christopher wrapped a strip of cloth around a gash on his shoulder caused by a near miss of the ogres club. "Cain't see how, rightly."

"We sure were lucky. And having the wolves there to attack right when we were too tired to do much more saved us for certain." Christopher said.

As Smarstick predicted, the wolves did indeed return. The group hardly heard them approach as the sky grew light in the east. The band of men and the pack of wolves were a strange sight, sitting in a circle together, discussing the attack.

"We chased him to the river." The once captive wolf said tiredly, for they'd been fighting and running for hours. "It was still dark, and he came on it suddenly. It's plain he didn't realize it was there. He yelled in surprise as he plunged in. The river is deep, and wide. He sank out of sight at once."

Smarlog explained what the wolves had seen. "Ogres ain't natural beasts.

They come from the roots of mountains. Oh, they're flesh and blood all right, but they didn't come ter life the way we know. It takes strong magic ter make an ogre. And like we've seen, it's clear that the ogre was looking for someone special." Eyeing the once captive wolf, he said "And thet makes me ask meself a few questions. How did the ogre know where we was? And who are ye, thet he would risk his own skin? Even an ogre prefers livin' over dyin' usually. And how did he know ye was all trussed up?"

"I cannot tell you how the ogre knew all that he knew," responded the wolf, "but I can tell you at least some of what he knew. It was apparent to no one more than to me that I was the reason he was here. Someone has reason to fear me. Perhaps someone was hoping that my death would break the agreement between us to show you to the Old Man of the Forest."

"I'd like to hear the answer to me other question." Smarlog pressed. "Who be ye that wolves will speak with humans to save ye, and ogres will risk all to try to kill ye? What makes ye so blasted important?"

The wolf looked over at his pack, and then at Smarstick, as if trying to come to a difficult decision. Finally, he looked back at Smarlog. "There's reason enough for wolf and man to distrust each other. But you here risked your very lives to save me tonight. And none less so than this little one, who turned the tide at the worst moment." He said, looking at Smarstick. "So I am going to tell you what no man has ever been told before."

There were barks and growls of concern from the pack, but the wolf turned to them and said "Our numbers dwindle. Our secret has not kept us safe ere now. Perhaps it is time to try a new way. I have decided, and must follow my heart."

Looking back at Smarlog, he resumed. "As you must already know, wolf packs are based on bonds between family members, and the occasional admission of outside members to strengthen our blood. What you could not know is that all wolf packs are also sworn in loyalty to one time-honored family, and this family is in return sworn to its leader, the Prince of the Wolves.

The reason that my brethren were willing to break a vow of silence that has lasted tens of thousands of years, is because by the wildest of chance, this boy here," he said, nodding towards Christopher, "managed to grab hold of the Prince back there in that crevice."

To everyone's surprise, Smarlog slapped his knee gleefully. "I swear, as serious as this all be, I can't help but laugh! It makes me wonder about a world run by kings that can be changed by the random act of a small boy!"

"Well, Prince, what now?" Smarlog asked with a more serious face. "I still think thet old man ye spoke of is the best place to git some answers. Fer all we know, he's the one what sent thet ogre our way."

"I agree, we must see the old man if he'll let us." replied the prince.

"Let us? By thunder, he'll have no choice if I git near 'im!" said Smarlog.

"Quite the point." Responded the Prince. "His magic is strong, and when he doesn't wish to be disturbed, you can somehow find yourself suddenly stepping through a glade on the other side of the forest, miles from where you were. But still, we must try, and somehow, I think he'll see us."

"One more thing." Added the prince. "In the heat of the battle, I was given my freedom by a dwarf that would have better served himself by getting out of the way of danger. I wish to repay that act."

The prince nodded to his pack, and three wolves stepped forward, with three very familiar packs hanging from their mouths. Each wolf strode to the proper owner, and handed the pack over. Smarlog sat on his log, somberly studying the pack for a long moment. Looking up, you could see a reflection in his eyes, as if tears were not far away.

"Wolf, ye've got an ally in the Smar clan!" he said with a raspy voice. "Lets go see this old man!"

7 THE OLD MAN OF THE FOREST

The band was now ready to move on. Once the wolves had rested sufficiently, they began the journey over the mountain range where the wolves said the Old Man of the Forest dwelt. The wolves knew the passes which would make the journey easiest, and led the way. All were greatly fatigued from the events of the past two days, and paths were steep, slowing the party's progress. By the end of that day they had not reached the middle pass so they stopped and camped. They slept quietly and this time, undisturbed.

They broke camp the following morning, with many grumbles of stiff muscles and aching wounds, even among the wolves. "I nivir thought about a wolf having a sense of humor before." Commented Smartwig to Christopher while watching the wolves as they came and went. "But they joke with each other jest like us when we're at our tasks. I heered one givin' another one jibes about not bein' able te catch a decent squirrel fer breakfast."

The rest of the trip over the mountain range was uneventful. Tired as they were, the men were taken with the raw beauty of the valley that unfolded before them as they reached the summit of the pass leading over the mountain. The view was brief though, for when they descended a few hundred feet they returned to dense stands of pines which blocked the valley from sight.

Quietly the band continued on. The walking loosened muscles stiff from the battle, and they made good time. But descending a peak uses different muscles than ascending one, and by the time they camped for the night they had traded one sore set of muscles for another, and their feet were tired and sore as well. At the foot of the mountains was a huge swamp dotted with enormous pine trees, and they had to pick their way through carefully to prevent sinking up to their hips in mud. Traveling through the swamp slowed their pace down greatly, and they began to get impatient. Smarlog also worried that they might not reach dry ground by the end of the day, and be forced to sleep in the swamp. However, they were able to reach higher ground just as light was fading from the sky. As soon as they reached a spot where the band could arrange a decent encampment (and that Smarlog proclaimed was a fair spot for defense in case of another attack) they started a fire and had a small meal. Most of the food they had packed was gone, since they had planned to replenish their supplies at the inn where they were not allowed to enter. But one of the wolves brought them a turkey he had caught, and they roasted bits of the meat over the campfire on sticks.

Early the following day, as they were continuing into the forest, Smarlog froze in place motioning the others to do likewise. Ahead of them through the trees they could see the huge unmistakable shape of an ogre.

Although the men had all halted, the wolves had continued on, as if they had not seen the brute. And the men watched in amazement as one of the wolves trotted between the legs of the ogre and continued on as if he had just passed another tree. The band moved closer, cautiously and slowly.

Number One noticed several of the wolves sitting up a hill to their left, tails wagging, and their mouths half open in a wolfish grin. Nudging Number Four, he pointed to them asking "What trick are they playin' on us now?" One of the wolves leaned forward and turned its head to the others and seemed to say something that the others found amusing because they all barked short laughs.

By now some of the other men had reached the ogre, and could see why the wolves were unafraid. This ogre had returned to his original state, which is to say he was made completely of stone. Number Six even took out his sword and tapped the chest of the ogre, causing the sword to ring like a chime.

Now the wolves trotted down from their observation post to share the joke with the humans. "And are you planning on doing battle with a rock, then?" one asked. Both wolves and men laughed this time.

"How did this happen?" Smartwig asked. "It's as if the magic that made him had been drained out!"

"There are more, too." The spokes-wolf said. "The Old Man of the Forest has told us that someone who does not like him very much occasionally sends these beasts to dispatch him. But they never leave the forest to return to their evil master, as you can see."

Sure enough, as they continued on they encountered more and more of these statues. Dozens of them, eventually. Some frozen in attack, some in retreat, but every one forever turned back to stone.

Eventually, the trail they now followed ended at a cave in a steep hill.

They all entered the clearing around the cave entrance and stood studying the cave quietly for a while. Now that they had reached their destination, the idea of confronting someone who had the power to turn dozens of ogres into stone seemed a bit over-ambitious. After all, the entire band had required the help of two dozen wolves to dispatch one of the monsters.

Still, the Smar clan was at stake so Smarlog stepped forward and called into the cave. "Old man! Old man! Ye have company, and some explainin' to do! Show yerself!"

"Well, well! You've arrived then! Splendid! What wonderful time you made! What a sturdy lot, then! Fantastic!" said a voice not from in the cave, and not from behind the band, but actually from a form now standing among the men and directly behind Christopher, who nearly jumped out of his cape. Turning to see the source of the voice he observed a man of average height, with a head of jet-black shaggy hair, and a big shaggy beard to match that seemed to stick out in any direction it pleased. He wore a tan cape of roughly woven cloth, and a shirt and pants of the same material but faded green in color. He wore no shoes, and his feet looked as though they were calloused enough to walk on hot coals.

Christopher also marveled at the man's bulk. For although he was no taller than the tallest farmer in the band of travelers, he seemed to be as big around as a one hundred year old oak tree, and his fingers were as thick as a good walking stick.

Despite the man's ominous bulk, Smarlog stepped up to him purposely. "I be Smarlog, of the Smar Clan." He began but was interrupted by the old man.

"Well of course you are, and a spittin' image of your great grandfather, too, if I do say so, myself." The old man proclaimed. "I'd know you anywhere."

"How could you have known my great grandfather? He passed on nearly a hunnert and fifty years ago!" Smarlog said. "Everybody knows men don't live as long as dwarfs, and you look a sight younger 'n me, and I'm over a hunnert now meself!"

"It's a fact, a fact indeed, Smarlog." The Old Man said. "And if I indeed were a man, then, why, you'd be more likely to find me by digging deep. But then, not everything is as it appears, now is it? And surely you remember tales in the halls of your own home as a lad, of a visitor, one who helped your clan escape certain destruction from the hands of the sorcerer, eh?"

"Visitor?" said Smarlog, with a startled look. "Sure, there were stories aplenty, of the one who came and conjured up an army from the rocks in the field outside the castle. It warn't enough to defeat the ogres, but it held 'em off til a good many of the survivors could escape, my family included. But yer not seriously suggestin' thet ye be the very one, are ye? Why, they say thet he was…"

"Brother to your attacker. Brother to the black Sorcerer." said the old man gravely. "Brothers, once, before he lost his soul to power. Long, long ago." he added in a sad voice.

"Before there were men. Yes, that is exactly what I'm suggesting. Not men, no, we are not men. Not as you know them, at least. We were an ancient race, with a very different path. Our people were fading away already, even before men began living together in villages. But our resemblance allowed us to blend in for eons."

Smarlog, not to be steered from the reason for their visit even by such a startling claim, decided to boldly confront the old man with his questions.

"Our name has been painted with a dark brush, and our friends here lied to." Smarlog said bluntly, motioning to the wolves who stood beside him. "We mean to know why ye told 'em we meant harm to their pack. What do ye say?"

With a sad smile, the old man sat back onto a tree stump. "I'll answer the question with a question." He said, looking at the big gray wolf leader. "Would you, Prince of Wolves, have purposely gone and broken your vow of silence, speaking to men or dwarves, simply because I appeared and told you that it would be in your interest?"

"No, of course not." Said the prince.

"Would you, Smarlog, have gone running off into the forest in search of wolves to talk to had I appeared to you at your campsite one night with the belief that they could be your ally?"

Frowning, Smarlog agreed "Not likely. We have a bone of our own to pick with someone, and cursed little time left to try."

Lifting his arms in front of him with his hands turned palms up, the old man said "As inappropriate as it may have seemed, I too had very few options, and 'cursed little time left'. My only hope of bringing your two forces together quickly enough was to thrust you together, and trust that cool heads would prevail. I do believe that other than this one time, I have not told a deliberate lie in the last ten thousand years. And I beg your forgiveness for having to have done it this time. Sometimes one does what one believes one must. Sometimes, your options are narrowed down to but one."

"But why?" Smarlog asked. "We were on our way to destroy the dragon, and reclaim our land. What is so important about our bein' here?"

"I'm afraid that destroying the dragon will not be enough, and I think you also suspect that. Your enemy has grown stronger over time, and has other minions to do his bidding, as you saw in the woods. For he was the one of course, who dropped that ogre into our forest to destroy the Prince before you two could reach an alliance."

"How do we know it was not you who sent that brute?" Number One spoke up.

"I think Smarlog will be able to confirm whose handiwork that was." The Old Man said softly.

"That ogre was ourn', all right, meanin' that it came from that blackheart." Smarlog said. "But it's not somethin' we're proud of. If we knew what they were a'fore he had us buildin' the parts…"

"We know the dwarves don't have the darkness of heart to dream up such a monster." The Old Man interrupted him gently.

"Smarlog, you know in your heart you need all the help you can get. I see you already found the boy." The old man said, holding Smarlogs gaze with his. Christopher's heart began racing again, and he felt a bit frustrated. How many blasted people around here know about him, anyway?

As if to answer the question, The Old Man went on. "That is a well kept secret. Even my brother is not sure if it is true, and other than the prophecy ages ago, no one speaks of it. But he who controls the dragon, the cloud and the ogres, and a band of sixteen against hundreds of ogres will not fare well no matter how stout your hearts. Surely you don't believe that the sorcerer will let you rebuild your castle in peace even if you do manage to defeat the dragon? Not after what you've seen these past few days?"

"But what can we do? Each day, he grows stronger, and we grow older." Smarlog said in exasperation. "And men aren't likely to band with us for no reason."

"True enough." Spoke the Old Man. "But you've begun to give them reason already, haven't you? Look at these twelve honest men you befriended. And while men are not in my debt, I have been of some use to some of their leaders in the past, and they will grant me council and hear me out. The sorcerer must be dealt with once and for all but we must be prepared, or we will lose the battle and the cloud will darken all the world we know. He began collecting his dark magic thousands of years ago, with the intent of remaining in this world forever, with whatever creatures remain at his beck and call. We two, my brother and I, are the last remaining members of our race to walk this world. The only reason I have stayed on this side as long as I have is because it is my duty to see he passes over with me. The time has come. If I fail, and am forced over without him, he will be the destroyer of your world."

The conversation continued on for some time after. The Old Man of the Forest had convinced the band that the danger was real, and that they must all work together to overcome the threat. In the end, as it grew dark once again, the band was told that they were welcome to the comforts afforded by the Old Man's cave, which turned out to be quite dry and cozy. Lighting candles inside, they began to settle down for the night.

Christopher had listened to all of this in absolute wonder. No one liked an exciting time more than he, but how could he be so unlucky as to land smack in the middle of such a disaster? The trials he'd been through so far were enough to make him wish he'd been pushed into an ice cream party instead of here. He'd been attacked by a band of men, nearly eaten by wolves, almost squashed by an ogre, and his feet were sore from walking more miles in the past week than he had in the prior year.

Sitting outside the cave on a rock, his head in his hands, he stared into a pool which collected at the side of the cave from a trickle of water that ran down the mountainside. He couldn't see very clearly, because his eyes were a bit watery. He was feeling scared and sad. What did he have to do with all this? What made him so important to winning this fight? And what if they were wrong? He missed his family terribly. He hadn't had a moment to think about them for days, but he wished they were all there with him now. His father, his mother, and especially his older brother. He'd feel a lot safer if _he_ were around to help take care of these ogres. Suddenly he noticed that the form of the Old Man was reflected in the pool of water. Looking up, he saw him standing there staring at Christopher with a kindly expression.

"I think we should take a walk and talk about your family." He said, as if he could read Christopher's thoughts.

They strode down a path where the trees almost seemed to step away in respect as they walked along. Christopher could hear running water, and they soon approached a waterfall which glowed in the fading twilight. They sat on boulders watching the erratic flight of bats as they came out to feed on the insects drawn to the moist pool.

"A boy your age must be very frightened by now with all the events going on." The Old Man said. "I bet your parents are searching high and low for you."

Tears began to run down Christopher's cheek. Until this point he had been busy enough not to think about it. "I'm afraid they may never find me. I have no way to tell them where I am, and they have no way to tell me where they are." He said. That was quite bad enough, but since they couldn't tell each other _when_ they were, he didn't see how he could ever find them.

"Oh, not necessarily." said the Old Man Mysteriously. "Why, I'm thinking you have actually left each other notes by now. You just didn't recognize the clues for what they were."

As if changing the subject, the old man said "You look familiar to me. I think I knew someone once, long ago, that you resemble. A lady who came by here with her husband. Thousands of years ago." Suddenly his eyes lit up, and he laughed loudly. "I was just remembering the way I met them! I was on the other side of the mountains from here, back the way you came from. He had just stumbled across the lair of a sabre toothed tiger, and ran past me like a startled rabbit! Oh, the look on his face! Ha!" He slapped his knee with the memory.

"He bounded past me and went up the cliff faster than a lizard! Just out of reach of the tiger's claws! Throwing chunks of rock he pulled out of the cliff until the cat gave up and went away. It struck me so funny I carved the scene in the cliff."

The story startled Christopher. Forgetting his sorrow for the moment, he asked "That was you that carved that scene?"

"As sure as I sit here now, it was." He replied. "And his wife, who had the sense to climb a tree long before the cat got close enough to be dangerous, well, you are the spitting image of her."

"Now how do you explain that, young one?" The Old man asked, studying Christopher from the corner of his eye.

Christopher gulped. But his desire to see his family was strong. "Right place, wrong time." He said glumly.

"Have you ever used a bow and arrow?" Asked the Old Man.

"Yes, what of it?" Christopher answered.

"Do you know how to find your range on a distant target?" The Old man pressed.

"Sure, it's easy." Christopher said to humor him. "Say your first shot falls short. Your next shot you adjust, and it usually falls past the target." Christopher's face brightened. "So the next time, you adjust the other way, and there you are!" He said brightly.

Smiling, the Old Man nodded. "I suppose finding a boy in time would work about the same way."

8 PARTING WAYS

The next morning, the band sat in the clearing outside the cave entrance discussing what to do next. The Old man walked over to the small pool of water where Christopher had sat in sorrow the night before. Turning to the band, he said "You need to see what you are up against. I know you realize now that it is more serious than you thought, but you need to see for yourself just how serious."

With that, he waved his hand over the water. It suddenly became milky, and they could not see the bottom. When it began to clear, instead of the bottom of the pool, they saw a range of hills.

Startled, Smarstick said "I recognize those hills! Those are around our old home!"

"They are indeed." The Old Man said. "Look closer."

The hills seemed to zoom toward them until they could make out trees and then other things on their peaks and sides. Some of the things on the hills were moving.

"Ogres!" Smarlog snarled. "Cursed beasts! Hunnerts of 'em!" He looked at the Old Man. "We'd have walked right into 'em if ye hadn't shown us. It's plain we need a plan. Hopeless or not, my fate is set. I am bound to return to me homeland and destroy thet dragon, or die tryin'."

"These men," he said waving his hand towards the farmers "have sworn they want to come and do what damage they can, to save their homes from the cloud. We could use some help, and ye've helped us find allies in these fine warriors" again a wave but this time towards the wolves. "But lookin' at them ogres, I'd say we ain't done needin' yet, and yer talk tells me that ye seem te think ye can fill thet need. What's on yer mind?"

"My plan is simple, and I think a simple plan has the best chance of success." The Old Man said. And with that, they bent their heads together - the dwarves, the men, the wolves and one small boy all listening intently as if their lives depended on it. For they surely did.

It was the plan of the Old man to travel now to a large settlement of men not far away. There he hoped to convince them of the dangers that had begun to amass on their borders. "It should not be too difficult. Their livestock begins to dwindle now, as yours once did." He said, nodding to the farmers. "I need your voices to help convince them. Will you come with me to tell them what happened with your homeland?"

"But what of the dwarves?" Number One asked. "They still need help."

"We can travel back the way we came and recruit more of the die-hards that may have stuck it out as you did." Smarlog said. "Surely more than twelve men survived yer kingdom."

"But I also want to leave Smarstick with the wolves." Smarlog said. "I think the dwarves need an ambassador with our new found allies, and I cain't think of a better one. I hold some secrets yet thet will be the end of thet dragon, and a smaller troupe has a better chance of comin' out of this forest unseen."

"And I shall send out messengers to our packs." said the Prince of the Wolves. "By the time the Old Man has arranged an alliance with the men from the settlement, we'll be ready to give aide as well. But warn the men that we will be coming, and in great numbers! They must be made to understand we'll work with them."

"Aye," The Old Man said, "I understand. And I pray that men have learned enough in this world by now to stand by the natural beasts and fight the unnatural ones."

"The cloud will be back soon, and when it does it will spell trouble." said the Prince of the Wolves. "My pack will stay here, for the moment. For it is certain that the cloud will bring more ogres. We can surprise them and cause confusion to keep them from discovering that you are all gone. But once we are ready we will march back south and west, toward the Sorcerer."

Christopher, Smarlog, and Smartwig now prepared to return the way they came. The most likely source of assistance would come from the dwindling settlements, along the road they had left behind days ago.

The Old Man replenished their food supply from his stores, and wished them well. "You may find that using my name will help win the confidences of the men you try to ally with. Tell them that I will be coming soon with their kin from the north, King Ammon and his army."

They wasted no more time, but set back off south towards the swamp. The wolves dispersed into the woods, and the Old Man and the band of farmers filed off towards the men's settlement two days away.

Christopher and the two dwarves, now rested, made good time reaching the foot of the mountain early enough to continue on and climbing to a secure lookout partway up the foot before settling down for the night. While not the spectacular view from the top, they could see out over the trees back the way they had just come. As the sun set to their left, the three sat on a ledge eating a cold hiker's dinner of dried fruits and nuts and looking towards the mountain and cliff where the Old Man's cave was hidden away.

They talked in muffled tones into the night about all the events they had experienced so far, and wondering what would come next. "Each step seems harder than the last." Christopher moaned. First we warm up on ogres, now the three of us go looking for a dragon! I hope you know what you're doing, Smarlog."

"Me too!" Smartwig said, pointing out a hawk to Smarlog and filching some of his dried fruit when he looked up.

"Me too." said Smarlog, pointing out a tree that was already starting to turn from green to gold, and filching some nuts from Smartwig when he looked.

Finally, the conversation slowed, then stopped, and the three moved back from the ledge and slept soundly under a pine tree. None of them noticed the owl that silently glided into the tree and sat as if on guard, while they slept.

When Christopher awoke the following morning, he thought it was still long before sunrise. But looking up, he could see no stars, and the two dwarves were already up. "The cloud?" he asked.

Smarlog nodded. Looking out over the valley back towards the cave, he said "I heard thet sound agin' last night too. Only it came and went, came and went, over an' over. Whatever it is, I fear it means trouble fer our friends."

Christopher knew that Smarlog must be worrying about his brother Smarstick too. He said nothing.

Suddenly, far off on the wind, they could hear the howling of wolves. "Thet would be the wolves setting up an attack, most likely." Said Smartwig, looking at Smarlog.

"We'd best be on our way. We got a job to do same's them." Smarlog said grimly.

Again they made good time, driven by an urge to see this task to the end. Each of them seemed to be more determined than ever. At the bottom of the mountain they angled to the southeast, by suggestion of the wolves, where they would find a river. The same river, in fact, that had brought the life of a very unlucky ogre to an untimely end quite recently. They hoped to find some fallen trees to tie together, and use the fast moving water to return them to the road more quickly. The road that they had traveled passed over this river near where they had met the farmers, and they had crossed it by bridge on the way to the inn.

They were successful in finding the river, and in finding trees. They were, however, less successful in not being found themselves. As they prepared their makeshift raft at the end of a small peninsula, they again heard the heavy tread of an ogre crashing through the woods toward them. Their raft was nearly ready to launch, and they had little choice but to push the logs into the water and jump aboard just as the ogre broke out of the trees and thundered toward them up the sandy spit of land.

Shouting in anger at being unable to reach them, the ogre trotted along the riverside tirelessly while the three did their best to guide the loosely tied logs down the river.

"If we make one mistake, we'll be history!" said Smarlog. "Keep yer eyes out. We need to either get away to the opposite side o' the river, or figger out a way to do 'im in."

As they passed under a thin tree, which had fallen completely across the river, Christopher said "I've got an idea. Let's see if I can get him out on this log. You two stay with the raft, but try to slow or stop around the next bend."

With that, he grabbed hold of two tree limbs as their raft passed underneath the tree, and clambered up. The ogre, seeing a clear path to his prey, immediately jumped onto the tree and strode purposefully towards Christopher. His balance was incredible, and his weight so great that the tree shook and shuddered and Christopher, although he was already half-way across the tree, was hard pressed to even get near the other side as the ogre smashed his way across. However, the further from the trunk, the smaller the limbs and the lower the tree bent. Now, the ogre's feet were underwater, and he began to have second thoughts. But it was too late. Christopher was still several feet from the other side when he heard the tell-tale cracking of wood, and he leaped in desperation. Grabbing an overhanging branch of a tree, he watched as the ogre sank to his hips, then his shoulders, then over his head, and out of sight.

Christopher's branch was not safe either, however, and his weight lowered it until he was bobbing in the water as well. It snapped suddenly and he drifted downstream. His pack was on his back and the extra weight pushed his head underwater. He kicked wildly, but could not bring his head back up. Looking up, he could see his outstretched arm as more and more of it submerged. Now he could see his whole hand underwater, and he was still dropping into the dark cold water when another hand broke the surface, grabbed his, and he was dragged upwards back towards the air.

As he resurfaced, coughing and gasping, he could hear Smarlog cheering. After grounding the raft around the bend, Smartwig had run back to see Christopher plunge into the river and quickly hung from a stout overhanging branch by his knees to catch Christopher as his submerged form drifted by.

Quickly the three clambered aboard the raft once again in case there were other ogres in the area, and slipped away. Christopher stripped off his cape and clothes and spread them out to dry. Smartwig handed him a dry blanket to keep warm under meanwhile. "To tell ye the truth, this be'ent sech a bad thing."

"No? I nearly got killed by an ogre, and then nearly drown. I don't see what's so good about that!" Said Christopher, wide-eyed at the near disaster he had just evaded.

From the other side of the raft, Smarlog said "Mebbe so, but ye were gettin' a bit ripe, anyhow."

Christopher stared at him a moment shivering, before replying with a grin "I'd like my bath a bit warmer next time, please. Thanks, Smartwig. I owe you one!"

Fortunately, the rest of their return to the road was uneventful and the fast moving river brought them to the bridge in half the time it would have taken to walk.

The trip did have one downside, though. Each was left with his own thoughts of those they'd left behind, and the memory of the wolf-howls in the wind, to remind them that their friends may not have been so lucky.

9 NEW ALLIES

As they approached the inn, they were greeted by the sight of 5 men in purple robes carrying a log toward the front door. Christopher assumed that they were bringing the log in for firewood. Remembering their unsuccessful attempt to enter the inn, he thought if he were helpful with this chore they would be more inclined to let them stay this time. And obviously, here was a great place to meet men who might be willing to help their cause. So he stepped boldly up to the front of the log, where there was plenty of room.

Reaching up, he put his hands under the log to support it and began to strike up a conversation with the men. "Having a good fire tonight, I see."

"The first man in line, whom Christopher could not see because he had his back to him, turned and smiled to the others. "Aye, we'll have a fair roast." The others behind him laughed.

"Maybe we'll roast some o' them Orange blighters inside, eh?" said the man at the back. There was another laugh.

"Orange who?" said Christopher.

"There are Orange men inside." Said the first man. "And I'll be hanged if I'll share an inn with an Orangeman!"

"So this log, it's not for the hearth?" Christopher asked as they neared the door.

"No, of course not! We aim to take the door down with it!" said the first man.

Inside the inn, Christopher could hear someone shouting "The Purplemen are back with a battering ram! Get ready to repel boarders!"

Smarlog and Smartwig had been walking alongside eyeing the men all this time.

"Ye oughtn't to get too involved in this til we sort out the apparent disagreement between these gentlemen and the others." Smarlog suggested.

42

"I agree," Said Christopher, "but we're looking for strong backs, and they certainly fit that category. I'd hate to see them get damaged before we can ask."

Smartwig winked at Christopher saying "Mebbe ye kin sorta help steer thet there ram so's to have the best effect, then."

Seeing the wink, Christopher said "I'll see what I can do." But there was little time to think, as they were now breaking into a trot to ram the door. At the last moment he did the only thing he could think of, which was to roll into a ball. The first man tripped over him, and the second over them, and then the third, and so on, until they were all piled up in front of the door and the log was rolling harmlessly away.

"What happened?" shouted the first man.

"Er, they ran out the back door!" yelled Smarlog.

The five burly Purplemen got to their feet and ran around the side of the inn as the peephole in the front door popped open.

"Where did they go?" Christopher heard a voice say.

"Excuse me sir, we'd like to come in please." He said.

"Come in? Highly unlikely just now, whoever you are! We are under attack, you know." said the voice.

"Yes sir, I do know. As a matter of fact, they should be coming in the back door right about now." said Christopher.

"Back door? Aaaaaaaaaaah!" shouted the voice. The front door flew open, and five men in dull orange robes burst out of the inn as if it were on fire.

Taking advantage of the open portal, Christopher and the two dwarves stepped inside to a momentary calm. The innkeeper sat in a chair blotting his forehead with a kerchief. "Nasty business, this Orange and Purple thing, eh?" he said. "Say, aren't you dwarves? I'm afraid I am not all that…"

His sentence was not completed, however, because the Purplemen were now banging on the back door loudly demanding entrance. Smartwig quickly closed the front door as Smarlog opened the back one. The five Purplemen burst in.

Looking around the room, some shouted "Where are they?" while others yelled "Let us at 'em!"

Smarlog quietly closed the back door, and stepped to the middle of the room. The apparent leader of the Purplemen strode up to him and reached down as if to grab him. Before he could reach Smarlog however, he was staring into a short sword, which was poking into the end of his bulbous nose. Staring cross-eyed at the blade, he slowly raised his hands. "Now, no need ter git techy, we was jest lookin' fer them no-good Orangemen what was here. We got no bone ter pick with you."

"Is that a fact, then?" said Smarlog, with a scowl. The Purpleman tried backing away but Smarlog matched his pace, stepping up on a chair, then onto a dining table and walking along its length until the Purpleman had backed himself right up to a wall. Smarlog now stood eye to eye with the man, his sword still poised.

"Fer someone without a bone to pick ye sure were quick enough to reach fer what ain't none o' yourn te touch. Now I suggest ye all five calm down til I get some answers here, or the Purplemen might jest have a nasty clan o' dwarves to answer to."

The four other purplemen had been mesmerized by the fact that their leader was so easily neutralized by such a small adversary. But now that it occurred to them that they perhaps should have been acting instead of observing, there were two other forms in between them and their leader, one gray haired dwarf, and one young boy. The dwarf looked small. But then so are bobcats, and you don't normally go getting them riled up. The boy leaned on a walking stick, but his hand rested on the hilt of a sword.

"So now thet you boys are in a talkative mood, let's hear exactly what makes ye think ye kin go around breakin' down the door o' this here honest innkeeper without so much as a how do you do, eh?" Smarlog asked.

The innkeeper had been as startled as the Purplemen when the dwarf took charge so easily. And given the apparent aggressive behavior of the Purplemen so far, he was not so sure he wanted to be pointed out. However, it was done and so he sat quietly, waiting to see what would come next.

"Well, he's housin' them blasted Orangemen an' thets enough fer me!" said the Purpleman, apparently warming up on his favorite subject.

"Oh, I see, so someone engaged in a perfectly acceptable practice sech as rentin' sleepin' quarters, or sellin' food, is a criminal, in yer eyes?" Smarlog pursued.

"Thet's right! Eh, I mean, well, no, o' course not, but..." stammered the Purpleman.

"But since you five law-abidin' door breakers were in the area, ye needed a good reason to cause havoc on this here road, and damage the only inn fer days in either direction, so's no other traveler could sleep safe tonight I suppose?" Smarlog snarled.

The Purpleman's eyes widened. "Now, thet's not it at all! Them Orangemen, they're always attackin' our settlements and kidnappin' folk and we end up payin' ransom te get 'em back."

"Not true! Not true!" came a muffled voice from outside the front door. Apparently, the Orangemen were still in front of the inn, and had been listening through the peephole which had been left unlatched. "Them Purplemen drive off our livestock and trample our crops, and when we can capture one o' their leaders, we do, to make them pay the damages!" One of them shouted.

"That raid o' yourn last week weren't on account o' no damage by us, ye orange coot!" Shouted the Purpleman.

"Was too!" yelled the voice right back. "Yer king's dang lama herd broke out inter our turnip fields two months ago, and what they didn't eat, your rotten lama-herders trampled whilst gettin' the herd back outta our fields. He never paid a single coin te cover our loss!"

"Thet's on account o' ye fools planted yer dang turnips where they had no business bein'!" shouted the Purpleman back. "Thet land was honored Purpleman land, where our ancestors once met each year fer harvest thanks."

"Yer fergettin' thet our ancestors met there too!" shouted the Orangeman.

Smartwig strode over and opened the door at this point, and grabbing the nearest orange robe, dragged the man inside. "I don't suppose you two are in anyway, er, related, are ye?" He asked.

"Bah! Not a chance!" fumed the Purpleman.

"Preposterous!" argued the Orangeman.

"Never!" added the Purpleman.

"We'd sooner cut out our own liver!" agreed the Orangeman.

"Well, maybe." said the Purpleman.

"Distantly." concurred the Orangeman.

"Long ago." added the Purpleman.

"Oh yes, way back." said the Orangman.

"And you two are…" Smartwig began the question.

"Cousins." said the Purpleman and Orangeman.

"Cousins." Smarlog said, shaking his head. Thank goodness ye ain't distant. I can't imagine how much ye'd hate each other then.

"Did the lamas really destroy the crop?" Asked the Purpleman, who was fond of the tubers.

"A good portion." Nodded the Orangeman. "Did we really plant them where the feasts used to be held?"

"Ye did."

Looking at Smarlog, the Purpleman said "I guess things sorta built up a momentum, there."

"This back and forth has got to take a toll on yer day to day chores, ain't it?" asked Smartwig.

"It's very trying." Said the Orangeman. "We spend a lot of time with our militia while our barns fall down around our ears."

"You kin say that agin, cousin!" agreed the Purpleman. "We lost two dozen pigs this year from untended fences! As if that cursed cloud an' them beastly ogres ain't enough to contend with!"

The conversation had gone so quickly to this point that Christopher could hardly keep up. But with this last comment, Smarlog and Smartwig stared at each other in concern about the Purpleman's comment on ogres. So Christopher used the chair as a step to the dining table as Smarlogn had and strode to the end of the table, up to the Purpleman. Slowly and mysteriously, he whispered loudly "Have we got a deal for you!"

It was clear that this feud had escalated over a long, long time between two settlements that were once closely related. It really did not take much to nudge them back towards helping each other rather than fighting each other. They were not mean men. They were dealing with new and frightening problems on their borders, and when one side or the other accidentally caused some initial damage (which side began it was unclear,) the feud began. It probably was a relief at the time, to react to something they understood. To fight over turnips, rather than ogres. But in their heart, both sides knew where the enemy lay.

So, the cousins reconciled. They shared the inn that night with the dwarves and Christopher and agreed to accompany them on their dangerous journey.

Sitting around the hearth, they all talked into the night. The dwarves and Christopher filled them in on their side-trip into the forest and over the mountains, and the men described the territory and how the ogres occasionally raided the Purplemen's outlying farms. As a result, they had the science of ogre fighting down pretty well. And it came to light that the Orangemen, who's land ranged close to the dwarves' old homeland, were familiar with the dwarves of old and their special magic. What's more, they were familiar with the doings of the dragon, and were willing to help the dwarves in laying their trap.

As scared as Christopher felt about what was to come, he couldn't help but feel elation that night. Up to now, even though they had been able to overcome each obstacle laid before them, it was only by the closest of margins. They had been on the defensive every moment. Now, they were about to go on the offensive. That night, he was able to forget his own sorrows, by losing himself in the hopes of these men and dwarves, who had lost so much more than he.

10 CAPTURED!

The mood the next morning was much more subdued, but no less hopeful. The innkeeper prepared breakfast and then disappeared, while the men ate quietly. Once they had finished they all turned to their belongings and examined them carefully. When walking into ogre country, it is best to know that your tools won't fail you. The five big Purplemen turned out to be armed with sledgehammers, the weapon of choice when on the fringes of their territory. "A nine pound hammer git's their attention a sight faster than a shout." explained one of the men to Christopher.

The Orangemen were not small men either, but a hammer is little defense against a dragon. They bore long spears, packs of mysterious tools, and a carefully earned knowledge of the land and the dragon as their chief weapons.

When the band was ready to depart, Smarlog looked about for the innkeeper. "Whar's he got off to? We need to settle up our bill and be gone afore long. Well, let's git our packs outside. Mebbe he's out workin' on the property."

They carried their packs outside, where they found the innkeeper carrying several bags of food to distribute to the group for their departure. He was now wearing a travelers robe like the rest of them and Christopher thought he saw a glint of sun reflecting off something under the open front. "I packed some extra food. You'll be needing it where you're going. There's not much left fit for a man out that way." He said, and then added "Or a dwarf. I want to apologize, Smarlog, up until I saw you get these two bands together, I'm afraid my opinion of dwarves was less than admirable. But It's plain you can't judge a book by its cover, and I'm not too proud of how I've acted these past few years here."

Smarlog frowned. "No sense grudgin, innkeeper. I appreciate yer honesty and wish ye the best. Havin' an inn what'll treat dwarves well hereabouts will be a boon to our clan once we've taken back what's ours. And the extra food will surely be appreciated in the days to come." Looking at Smartwig who was already examining the bags of food for snacks, he added "Mebbe sooner."

Then, noticing the innkeeper's garb, he asked "What's this, though, ye be goin' away too?"

The innkeeper looked sheepish. "There was a time that I was more than an innkeeper. I served for years in the king's army to the north. I thought you might just be able to use another hand, and the way things are, this inn won't make me much of a living until that gang is taken care of. And I come fully outfitted, it'll cost ye nothing."

With that, he spread open his robe to show a chainmail shirt, leather breaches, and a well used but very serviceable long sword buckled about his waist.

"I'm not the young man I once was, but I still know what I'm doing in a fray." He added.

Smiling, Smarlog replied "We're ten men, two dwarves and a boy off to take on dragons, ogres, and who knows what else. I reckon we got room fer one more."

Now the men headed west. But this time, they did not stroll down the middle of the road as they had in the past. While they followed the direction of the road, they also kept off the road and inside the edge of the forest, hoping to escape notice as they penetrated the lands where the sorcerer's power was strengthening. "Likely, he's got eyes hereabouts." Smarlog said. "The less we're noticed the better."

It rained that night, a dark greasy rain. They found an old oxcart abandoned on the side of the road. They crawled underneath, and huddled close, to keep warm and dry.

As they lay there, the two dwarves and Christopher wondered what had transpired back in the forest. The cart was high enough that these three could sit up. "We need to know if there was a battle, and how it went. It could mean the difference between success and failure." Smarlog said. "We've got to find out somehow."

"How?" Smartwig asked between bites of dried fruit. "We'd need a good pair of eyes to see thet far."

"Maybe I can find aid." Said Christopher, but he would say no more.

The next morning, the clouds were gone and the bright early autumn sun shone on the land. The air was cool and clean, from the north, a harbinger of the winter to come.

It was decided that it was too risky for the entire band to move forward without scouting out the territory. Smartwig and one of the Orangemen volunteered to go ahead, and find the best way to approach the old castle where the dragon now lived.

"It's about another day out, if I recollect right." Smartwig said. The Orangeman agreed but added "Mebbe a tad longer, if we needs te travel careful." Hearing this, Smartwig added more food to his pack.

The Purplemen and the remaining Orangemen decided to move to the safety of the trees for the day and Smarlog announced he would scout the local terrain, in case there was trouble brewing.

Christopher said he would see what he could learn about their friends if he could, and walked out to the middle of an abandoned turnip field where he sat quietly, his dull green cape blending in with the dried weeds. Once again he spoke the words that brought the falcon to life on his walking stick. Once again the bird blinked and looked around, cocking his head at Christopher.

"I need the eyes of a bird." Christopher said. "A hunter. Someone we can trust. Someone who can travel far and fast, and bring us back news of our friends."

Blinking, the falcon spoke. "There is such a one nearby."

Startled, Christopher said "How can you know so fast?"

"I see him. I recognize him." He replied.

"Recognize? Who? Where?" Said Christopher.

"Over your right shoulder, where good friends stand." The falcon head answered.

Looking over his shoulder to the edge of the field, Christopher could see nothing. "I don't see him. Can you summon him?"

The falcon's reply was a shrill and short burst of three whistling calls. Suddenly from the tree tops, Christopher saw movement. A small shape swooped down to the level of the grasses in the field and began to slowly glide near. Once in the open, Christopher eyes widened in recognition. "Heart!" He whispered.

His old friend glided to his right shoulder, and perched. "Ouch! Watch those talons! What are you doing here? Have you followed me all this time?" He asked.

Heart rubbed his head against Christopher's cheek in response.

The falcon asked "What would you have him do?"

Christopher explained their belief that there was a battle after they left the Old Man of the Forest. "We need to know the outcome."

Heart nipped Christopher's ear and was off in a silent flurry of feathers. "Wait here." The falcon said. "So Heart can find you easily on his return."

So Christopher spent the day sitting in the field, afraid to move, for fear of losing his friend.

When Smarlog returned from his rounds, he sat with the men under the trees who had been watching Christopher. "He's talkin' to birds out there now!" said one.

"Eh?" asked Smarlog.

"He called one in from the trees! An owl, it was. We seen it glide right over an' sit on 'im!"

"You don't say!" Said Smarlog, smiling, and remembering Smartwig falling backward from the sight of an owl on his plate of sausages. "He's got a few surprises now and then, thet boy."

In the late afternoon, while Christopher was fidgeting and trying to get two crickets he'd caught to race each other around his legs, the falcon suddenly spoke again. "Be still. We are watched."

Christopher froze where he was, hoping his old green cloak would be enough camouflage to confuse any watchers. "Who's watching? Where are they?"

The falcon replied, "Far, far up. Above the clouds. A dragon heads east."

Christopher's blood ran cold. If the dragon made him out, he was toast! Literally! He lay there, unmoving, for what seemed an hour. Finally, the falcon said "Tis' safe now, he is behind the clouds."

Christopher realized he had been holding his breath, and let it out in relief. He noticed his hands were shaking, and he wished Heart would return.

But it wasn't until the sun was nearly done setting that the small ghostly shape appeared out of nowhere only yards away and swooped back onto Christopher's shoulder. This time Christopher didn't complain about the pinching.

But the news was not all good. There was evidence of a great battle in the forest valley. Heart described the scene as "Shattered ogres and wolf fur everywhere." according to the falcon. It did look like the Old Man of the Forest and a number of men made it over the river to relative safety eventually. Several ogres had fallen into the river and drown, as evidenced by the river taking a new path, as though obstructed by huge rocks.

Looking at the damage done to the forest, Heart thought someone might have been captured, but couldn't be sure. He couldn't find any of the remaining attackers close by.

When the sky darkened completely, Christopher made his way back to the band under the trees to give Smarlog the news. He decided to let the falcon remain awake from now on. An extra pair of eyes might come in handy. Heart swooped off to find dinner.

Smartwig had not yet returned. They sat around a tiny fire, afraid to cast too much light in this territory. Their concern was evident in how they chose to sit. They encircled the flames, but sat facing away from the fire, peering into the dark. Christopher told Smarlog what Heart had learned.

"I worry most thet one of our party might be captured. It's clear the sorcerer has eyes in the forest, as dim as they may be, or he wouldn't have been able to send the ogre at us. I think this attack were to larn more of what we're about." Smarlog said. "If I were him, I'd know thet the only way to know fer sure, is to ask. And thet means he needs someone to ask. And since he ain't about to wander out and say 'pretty please', I bet the attack were to collect 'im someone to talk to. Thet's the only reason I can figger so many ogres'd be so fer away. What I don't get is how they get there so blasted quick. But there's one thing I kin do, and thet's to use a little o' thet cursed sorcerer's own magic to look fer trouble."

Smartwig and his companion returned midway through the following morning. Crouching down at a patch of mud, he drew a rough sketch of the castle. It showed where the dragon had broken through a roof and part of an upper wall to gain entrance to the main hall. "He be too big to enter the main gate. When they stormed the castle, it were him what made the breach. Once the ogres got in the main hall, all was lost." He explained to the men.

"How big is the hole, Smartwig?" asked Smarlog.

"Jest about the size we guessed." Smiled Smartwig grimly. "It'll do the trick sure enough."

Looking at the Orangemen, Smarlog said "I'm goin' to need some stout hearts, though, to carry out our plan. If we're seen, or heard, we'll be naught but a well-cooked snack."

Suddenly Smarlog stood up. In anguish, he said "There's one more thing. I've been agonizin' over this all night. I may be able to larn if any of our friends are captured. But it's mighty risky. The Sorcerer is sure to feel the magic I use, since it were once his. It may give the game away. He won't know fer sure who we are, or where, but he'll know we be lookin'. And he's likely to guess it be the Smar clan's doin'. But we need to know if the plan is in jeopardy."

He then pulled a small bundle from his bag. It was the size of a baseball, wrapped in a red cloth. He unwrapped the object carefully to reveal what appeared to be a huge red gem. Laying the cloth out on the ground, he placed the gem in the center. Next, he produced a small wand from his pack, and waving it back and forth slowly over the gem, spoke quietly in a tongue that Christopher had never heard before. Before long, the gem began to glow faintly, and seemed to grow until it covered the entire cloth. Suddenly, movement could be seen in the gem. Fascinated, the band all watched as the movement clarified into a moving picture of two ogres, each with a limp form slung over their shoulders, rapidly walking through the brush. From time to time they looked over their shoulders, as if they might be pursued. Briefly the picture cleared even more, and Christopher gasped. "Smarstick!"

"And the other be the Prince of Wolves, no doubt!" said Smarlog. "And look whar' they be headin'! Right smack into thet dark-hearted villain's lair!"

Sure enough, a castle on a mountainside, could be seen beyond the ogres. "I'd know the skyline o' thet castle anywhar. This couldn't be worse. We must move quickly now, before he larns what we're a'doin!"

Christopher and Smartwig watched Smarstick and the Prince of wolves bobbing limply on the ogres shoulders until the view in the gem faded to a dull blood red. Then they stared at each other for a long, long, moment.

"Cain't leave 'em, now can we?" Smartwig said.

"Nope." sighed Christopher.

11 SPREADING THE NEWS

The old man of the forest seemed out of place in the great hall where he now sat. He was still garbed in forest greens, with his tan traveling robe beside him on another chair. He was also still barefoot. He looked very tired, and his clothes were stained from the struggle he and the men had been through.

The band of farmers looked tired too but even so, they continued to stand shoulder to shoulder in a circle behind the Old man.

In comparison, the group faced a very fit looking middle-aged man with long brown hair, dressed in silk clothing. His dark green shirt was embroidered with silver and gold thread, and he wore highly polished black boots that came up to his knees. The hall was decorated with beautiful hangings, and was lit up by highly polished chandeliers with pure white candles.

"I thank you for your hospitality, King Ammon. And I apologize for the short notice with which we have thrust ourselves upon you. But our mission here is very important, or we would not have requested an audience so abruptly."

"I never doubted that your reason for requesting an audience was a good one." said the king. "And I always look forward to seeing you again although I must admit, we usually meet only when something bad is about to happen."

He looked questioningly at the band of farmers behind the Old Man, but no one offered an explanation quite yet and they managed to maintain calm unreadable expressions.

The Old Man of the Forest smiled and agreed with the king's words. "It's true enough, that I often come when wrong must be righted, but there have also been times when my presence was appreciated by your people too."

"I never meant to imply otherwise, Old Man. I only point out that your appearance tends to be a harbinger of calamity. Or are you going to tell me that you are here only to visit, this time?" he said, putting an innocent look on his face.

"I wish that I were, and that my visitation was simply to invite you to accompany us on a quiet, peaceful journey. However, this time I come as an emissary. You have neighbors who have been buffering your country for many years and who are asking that you consider an alliance with them. Some of these others seem unrelated and unlikely allies, but I believe we can convince you that this would be in your best interest."

"An alliance, eh? Hmm. When kingdoms talk of allying themselves in times of peace, the smell of war is usually not far away. But, we border no lands where men are in such turmoil. All our problems these days tend to lie towards the southwest whence comes that cursed greasy rain and occasional wild stories about men of stone and such. But those territories are sparsely populated no-man's lands. So what are you proposing, Old Man? And whom do you represent?"

"Ah, there are more kingdoms around you than you'd ever supposed, Your Majesty." began the Old Man of the Forest.

"Oh, I hate it when you start using those high-minded titles! It never means good news! Spit it out man, I promise that I'll listen. Have you ever known me not to be fair minded?"

And so, slowly, from the beginning, the old man explained as well as he could to King Ammon exactly what was occurring. He worked his way through history, and then illuminated the dangers. The Old Man explained that those "sparsely populated no-man's lands" actually were defined kingdoms, even though they were not as organized as this one. When the Old Man spoke of the Purplemen and the Orangemen, this did not surprise the king either, for he knew of them. But when the story turned to the history of the dwarves, King Ammon's eyes widened. Of course he'd heard of them but their land did not border his, and at any rate, they were gone from the territory before his people settled here. So he and his people had never seen them and they just assumed these were old wives tales.

Now the Old Man spoke of ogres, and the king's jaw began to drop open. He went from staring in wonder at the Old Man, to glaring in anger at his advisors - highly paid men who should have been keeping him informed of such incredible border activities.

His advisors spent as much time as the king with their jaws hanging in amazement, but the king's stares made them look about and dab the perspiration from their foreheads with silken handkerchiefs.

By the time The Old Man of the Forest got to the dragon, King Ammon could not contain himself any longer.

"Stop! Surely you've lost your mind! Each story you've spun here is harder to take than the last! Dragons? And how do you propose that I inform my generals we must march on mythical creatures?"

"Oh, as for the ogres, you've heard the rumors. I can tell by your earlier mention of men of stone that you have heard at least some of this, although not all. Ogres are sometimes referred to as men of stone, for they come from the bones of mountains. And as for the dragon, you don't really have to march on that for he resides in the dwarves' castle to the west and to the north of the Sorcerers castle. The dwarves have taken the task of his demise to hand since they were actually the original creators."

"Oh, thank you very much! So I can tell my generals to ignore the mythical dragon, because the little people are going to do him in! Old Man, sometimes you make my job so hard!" the King said in exasperation.

Turning to the guard at the door, he shouted "Get me the sergeant at arms!"

Then, looking at his advisors he roared "And I'd better hear a good reason why the men of stone weren't investigated before this! I suggest you three get out there and collect enough information on any and all of this as you can, and hope it's enough to save your skins, let alone your jobs!"

The advisors did not need any further encouragement, but bolted for the exit.

Now bringing his attention back to The Old Man of the Forest, the king said "Surely you haven't come here without some proof of your own, have you?"

"Well," replied the Old Man, "let's see. There are the dozens of ogres that have been returned to stone near my humble abode back in the forest valley. For starters, you could send scouts there. Oh, but warn them to be on the lookout, there may be more wandering the forest. Yes, be very careful. Actually, you might do well to set more guards at your southern border, today. Oh, and arm them with sledge hammers, I think." He looked up at the farmers questioningly. They nodded their agreement silently.

The King's eyebrows went up, looking back and forth between the farmers and the Old Man. "Your home? So close to our border?" Slamming his fist on the table he rose up in agitation and began pacing. "What else haven't you told me yet?" He asked.

Now the Old Man of the Forest explained as best he could about his brother, the black sorcerer, who controlled the ogres and the dragon and his plan to enslave his neighbors and stay in power forever. King Ammon sat back down, staring at the Old Man in wonderment.

"You are just full of surprises today." He said. "Besides the fact that we have a land sparsely populated by burly farmers with big hammers ready to fight ogres, and an army of dwarves closing in on a castle with a dragon in it, what other good news have you brought me?"

"Well," The Old Man started slowly, "Actually, there was one more thing. There is another ally, which I haven't mentioned yet."

"Wonderful!" said the King wryly. "And what fairy creatures might these be?"

"Oh, no, no! They're quite natural! Yes, quite so! As natural as the forest, I'd say." said the Old Man with a grin. "Oh, yes indeed. But we really need to talk about them some more. You may have some trouble with this one…"

"Oh, come now!" roared the king. "What more could you possibly come up with that I would have trouble believing? Dragons, ogres, dwarves! Please!"

At this point, the Sergeant At Arms stepped into the room as he had been bidden and saluted. "Yes, Your Excellency? I am come as commanded." he said, saluting, after a rather tardy pageboy, whose job it was to announce people entering the room had jumped up and shouted "The Sergeant at Arms!"

Holding his head, the king groaned "Thank you, very much."

The pageboy stammered an apology. "Sorry Your Excellency, Sir, it's just that I, I've never heard quite so much news all at once, and …"

"Oh, never mind! This whole day has pretty much knocked us all off balance, eh?" the King said.

Quickly now, the king explained to the Sergeant that he needed some men to scout the outlying territories. "Send messages to our farthest outposts to gather the truth about this. I want answers by the day after tomorrow at the very latest! As a matter of fact, I want my first report by the morning!" He said.

Astounded, the Sergeant stammered "Surely, Your Excellency, you can't believe that this could be true! Ogres?"

King Ammon looked at The Old Man of the Forest and said "You know, if it were anyone else before me now, including my own kin, (no, especially my own kin!) I would declare them as mad as a March hare and have them locked up for their own protection. But this man's words have born truth before, and this won't be the first time that his stories seemed too much to believe. I do hope he's wrong, but I won't place any bets on it just yet."

The Sergeant at Arms saluted smartly and, spinning about, left the room to carry out the orders. Meanwhile King Ammon turned his attention back to The Old Man of the Forest. "Now where were we? Oh yes, I'm sorry. You were just about to tell me all about some new allies you'd found for me, weren't you?"

Instead of speaking, The Old Man of the Forest stood up and put his hand on the shoulder of Number One. The King's eyebrows raised again in question, but he stood silently waiting.

The farmers now stepped apart, opening the circle that they had maintained even as they walked into the room as a group.

At first, the king did not understand. Then his eyes slowly drifted down to the three forms in the center of the circle. Staring back, straight into his eyes, were three huge gray wolves.

One stepped forward, and said "We're pleased to make your acquaintance, Your Excellency."

"I need water." The King croaked, as he sat back down.

12 ON THE MOVE

Two days later king Ammon had more than enough information to convince him that the threat was real. He called his generals together, and they immediately began preparing plans, and ordered their lieutenants to ready the troops.

The first thing they needed to know was exactly what their enemy could do. So calling their best 40 scouts into a special meeting, the generals filled them in on the perils of the area they would be invading and then sent them off into the sorcerers territory with very explicit instructions. This meeting was well guarded, and the scouts were warned not to tell anyone their plan or to speak to anyone of the three gray emissaries they met in the meeting.

Of course Christopher and Smartwig, back in the forests west of the inn, knew nothing of these plans. After the fateful vision of Smarstick and the Prince of Wolves in the magical red gem, they had decided to set off on their own to see if they could rescue them.

Smarlog had argued with them as they packed and readied themselves, but they were not to be dissuaded. "Yer riskin' everything! Cain't ye see? I need every man I kin git! I used the ogre stone! The Sorcerer is sure to know somethin's afoot! An' what about the prophecy?"

But Smartwig knew the old stories as well as anyone. "No one ever said the boy would git the dragon, Smarlog. They said he'd turn the tide. We don't know what thet meant. Fer all we know, it meant he'll rescue our brother afore they break 'im."

Christopher felt like he wasn't there, the way they discussed him. And their putting so much importance on him scared him nearly to death. In a way, he preferred going towards the sorcerer's castle to the risk of failing at defeating the dragon, and being held responsible for the loss of the dwarves' homeland. On the other hand, this new thought, that he'd somehow snatch Smarstick from the heart of the sorcerer's lair like some sort of super hero had him even more worried. It seemed like no matter what direction he went in, everyone believed he was going to save them all. Everyone, that is, but him.

He certainly felt sorry for Smarlog, who as leader of the Smar clan was forced to put saving his people ahead of saving his brother. Smarlog had been a great education to Christopher since they met. Here was someone who had made it clear what the difference was between being in charge, and being a leader.

Christopher had no such responsibility, nor did he want it. Smartwig, for his part, was sworn to protect the clan as well. But he did not wear the heavy cloak of leadership, and he argued that saving his brother was also saving the clan in a way, even if it was one dwarf at a time.

If the truth were known, Smarlog might have argued harder, but he was grateful that the two were willing to try to save Smarstick, whom he loved every bit as much as Smartwig did.

So the two now trotted towards the castle keeping to old animal trails and with a sharp eye for patrolling ogres, who became more and more prominent as they neared the hills. So much so, that their hope of catching up with the captives before they entered the castle walls faded within a few hours. But still they moved on.

In the afternoon they found themselves constantly climbing and often could glimpse the castle walls. They kept low, since only sickly short bushes grew along the hillsides and they feared being seen by guards on the walls. But they were still quite a distance from the front gate, and the high number of patrols they kept having to dodge and hide from forced them to skirt around to the north side of the castle in hopes of finding a less guarded side entrance.

This seemed to be possible, and at any rate, the number of patrols did drop off significantly, the further from the main road they traveled. Eventually, they found themselves due north of the castle when yet another patrol caused them to suddenly dodge around a small cliff face covered with a dark greasy ivy. Quietly wiggling their way into the vines, they stood watching as three ogres passed within a few yards of them.

"We'd best be headin' in towards the walls now, te' see if'n these critters left a door ajar." Smartwig said. But before they could move, there was a sudden puff of air from behind them, which startled the two.

"Say, did you feel that?" asked Christopher.

"Sure enough, I did!" said Smartwig. "But air don't normally come from a rocky cliff! Let's see what we're up agin', here."

Slowly and quietly, the two crawled deeper into the curtain of vines, towards the cliff, until their heads poked out of the growth, into cool darkness.

"I think there's a cave here." whispered Christopher, feeling his way forward on his hands and knees until he was completely clear of the vines. Smarlog waited quietly for Christopher's report.

Christopher felt his way from the floor of this discovery up the right hand side, and then over his head. He could just reach the ceiling if he stood on his toes. Then he worked his way around down the left side, back to the floor. Then he crawled back to Smarlog. "It's perfectly round!" he said. "Like a tube. Like a straw. And smooth as glass! Someone had to have made this, but I don't see how."

"Likely a little dwarfish insurance, I'd say." answered Smartwig. "When the sorcerer attacked and enslaved our people, we were forced te' re-enforce his castle, but mebbe he don't know everythin' we done."

"It's been a long time, Smartwig. Even if this was a secret when it was dug, he might have found out by now." Christopher reminded him.

"But right now, it's the only option. We don't have naught to lose by investigatin'." Smartwig replied.

So Christopher wiggled his way back through the vines to plant his walking stick in the dirt at the outer vines as a lookout, much as he'd done when they had tracked the wolves to the crevice in the cliff in the forest. Then crawling back, the two stepped slowly along into the depths single file. Christopher went first, followed closely by Smartwig. Since they had no source of light, Christopher instinctively walked with his hands in front of him and Smartwig walked behind, keeping a hand on his shoulder. They moved forward for hours without change. The cave did seem to worm back and forth somewhat, although they could not tell how much in the dark. However, it neither climbed nor descended and they felt they must be very far below the castle. Eventually, they grew tired and hungry, and decided to stop to eat and rest for the night.

They were not the only ones settling down and finishing a cold meal. At the same time King Ammon's army, which had been traveling south at a rapid pace, was setting out pickets to guard against ogre attack and setting up an encampment. "Warn the men not to break out too much gear." King Ammon told his generals. "We march before daybreak. We have far to go and quickly."

There are times when travel is best done at night. Smarlog, with the innkeeper, the Purplemen, and the Orangemen, had moved along northwestward towards Smarlog's ancient ancestral homelands. Eventually, they came to the edge of the forest, where they could actually see the skyline of the dwarf's old castle off in the distance. There they waited under cover of the trees until dark. When they could hardly see each other in the dark, they began a long and slow journey across the plain that separated them from the castle.

Coming upon a deep gulley, Smarlog instructed them to climb to the bottom. "This here slash runs fer quite a spell west by northwest. It'll git us closer in without the chance of bein' seen. At the other end, we'll be southwest o' the castle. We kin reconnoiter the ground around it from there."

So as quietly as they could, they slid to the bottom and walked along the trickling stream which fed stunted shrubs that still managed to survive the ravages to the land caused by the dragon raking up the ground, and by the choking soot that the black cloud brought.

"This were a beautiful land, once, innkeeper." Smarlog whispered. "I wish ye could've seen it then.

"Perhaps I'll stay and help you rebuild after we're done with this mess." He whispered back. "I did miss the road once I'd settled at the inn, and I suddenly feel like I used to. Like I have a purpose again!"

The innkeepers reply had a lifting effect on Smarlog, who, even though he'd taken on this mission without allowing the thought of failure to enter his mind, couldn't help but wonder about the outcome. For the sake of all, he hoped they could manage to pull this off. Even great leaders have moments of uncertainty.

As he walked further, his mind wandered to his brothers and Christopher, now far to the south. He wondered how they were faring, and his thoughts grew as dark as the cloud.

By daybreak, the band was at the far end of the gully and all they could do for the time being was study the landscape so they would be prepared for the following night. After a time, they slid back down to the bottom of the gully and waited.

13 TESTING THE ENEMY

King Ammon's forty scouts were the very best at what they did, and none were better than Gralbin who nearly seemed to disappear when he wanted to remain unnoticed. The instructions at the meeting were very precise, and he intended to follow them to the letter. Like the rest of the scouts, he had ventured deep into dangerous enemy territory, where he found and trailed a lone ogre. All day long, he had stayed within a rocks throw of this beast without being noticed. At times he was close enough to hear him breath, and often to smell his rancid breath.

At the exact moment during the day that King Ammon had told them to expose themselves, he chose a branch of the shrub he was hiding behind, and slowly bent it, until it made the faintest of crackling. The ogre's head jerked up and he looked around. "He must have the hearing of a hound!" thought Gralbin. Then he silently moved upwind of the ogre, and within seconds, the ogre had caught his scent on the slow breeze. With a bound, the ogre was nearly on Gralbin before he could move, but his lightning fast reflexes saved him, and he managed to duck under the ogre's great arms and run past him. Keeping his pace exactly the same speed as the ogre's, he now allowed himself to be chased back towards his kingdom, as if frightened away.

The sorcerer was now sending out so many ogres so far, that King Ammon believed that they were instructed to capture anyone found in his territory at all costs. And it appeared that he was correct.

So precise was the timing of the scouts, that all forty ogres being followed spotted their decoy within five minutes of the same moment. This was a risky maneuver for the scouts, since they had to run back the entire distance with a tireless ogre not too far behind them, but they were wonderful athletes and could actually have outpaced the ogres and disappeared.

However, they did have to keep a sharp eye out so they didn't stumble upon another ogre on the way back and be accidentally cut off from escape.

On and on Gralbin ran, for hours. Eventually, he began to glimpse some of the other thirty nine scouts and could see that each was dutifully being chased back by an ogre of his own. It could be said that the sight of forty ogres running after them may have provided the scouts with an additional reason to run well.

Finally, the scouts ran into a wooded pass in the hills and seemed to disappear from sight. The ogres continued their pursuit, certain that they could not be far. Once all the ogres had entered the woods, they met King Ammon's ambush.

There came shouts from in front and to both sides of them. Finally, there were shouts from above as well. Some of King Ammon's soldiers had climbed the ancient oak trees that made up these woods and hauled great boulders up behind them, which they now dropped on the startled ogres with great precision.

But ogres are not pacified easily. Perhaps it is safe to say that ogres are not pacified at all. In a rage, they fell to defending themselves against their attackers, swinging their vicious clubs and even picking up some of the boulders that had dropped on their heads, and tossing them back at the oncoming army.

King Ammon had laid his trap well, and the outcome was only a matter of time. But that is not to say that his army went away unscathed, which is the sadness of war.

The army took to the ogres with sledgehammers and long spears, and the battle raged for hours. Roars shook the trees as the battle raged one way, then another, as the ogres tried every direction to break out of the deadly trap. In the end, as the sun set blood red in the western sky, thirty-eight of the ogres had been destroyed. The remaining two made an insane charge at their foes, sweeping soldiers away with the ends of their clubs as they ran and broke through King Ammon's lines, running through the forest.

By chance, their path led them into the band of farmers - Numbers One through Twelve - and the Old Man of the Forest. The farmers immediately prepared to attack. But the Old Man stepped in between them, and summoning all of his magical strength, raised his hands as he spoke seven magic words in a thunderous voice. Words that no human had ever heard before, and that ogres only hear once. At the end of the seventh word, he sank to his knees in fatigue. "Stoning" two ogres at once takes a bit of energy.

The two ogres slowly stiffened, and turned gray. Finally, they stood there, unmoving. Newly formed granite statues, attesting to the terrible battle that was fought there that day.

Such a battle could not go unnoticed, and there were slithery, crawly creatures in the employ of the sorcerer, who witnessed the scene. As a dull quiet now settled over the army, these spies began the trek back, to warn the sorcerer that the army of men now knew of his minions and may be on their way soon.

As for King Ammon's army, they now tended their wounded, and buried their dead. For when forty ogres mean to do damage, not all men can survive. Not even well trained ones. That night, King Ammon assembled his men, and thanked them for their bravery and ferocity, and swore that this battle would never be forgotten by free men.

As a matter of fact, that area became known in years to come as the forty ogre wood, and was a reminder of the day that men learned for certain that the sorcerer and his plans were not just wives tales, but were indeed terribly real.

Finally, with the work done, the army laid down to rest for a short time. Tomorrow would be even harder. But King Ammon had learned what he needed, and sent messengers to his outlying commanders, with instructions on what they would need to do and what special equipment they should prepare.

None of the sounds of the great battle had reached the ears of Christopher and Smartwig who, by the time it had begun, had risen from their own camp (even if it was in the belly of a mountain) and for quite some time journeyed onward. They had been in darkness for so long, they debated whether they should continue on at all or turn back and try another route. But finally, they decided to see where this ended and hope their luck would hold out just a little bit longer.

Spending two days in total darkness, and never being certain whether you might walk smack into an ogre without even knowing it until it is too late, can be very trying. Christopher was as jittery as a turkey on Thanksgiving, and Smartwig was eating even faster than usual.

When finally they came to the end of the tunnel, it ended in a shaft thirty feet across that went straight up. Stairs, without any railing, spiraled around the shaft up and out of sight. Keeping very close to the wall they slowly worked their way up the shaft, growing more and more nervous about the great distance between them and the bottom of the shaft should they slip or lose their balance. They lost track of time as they climbed, but it had to be hours that they ascended those stairs, growing quite tired from the repetitious walk. Finally, they could see the top of the shaft, and treading even more quietly, stepped up to the landing.

A dim light came from overhead. Reaching up, Christopher could feel a square grate about a yard across.

"Must be a trap door." Smartwig whispered. Thar ain't no door in the two walls here, and surely they don't jest step off 'n plummet."

The trap door did not budge, however, so Christopher drew his knife and using it as a wedge and crowbar, began working his way around the entire square. "Probably hasn't been used in a thousand years." He whispered back to Smartwig."

"Thet's good!" replied Smartwig. "Thet mean's they ain't awaitin' fer us on t' other side."

At the same time that Christopher's knife was working it's way around the trap door, Smarlog was preparing for the final approach to the castle wall across the northern plain. The sun had just disappeared and in the darkening twilight, the band slipped out of the gully and moved slowly and cautiously towards the old dwarf castle. A half moon hung in the southern sky, and they kept close to what brush and shrubs were available, to mask their approach.

On the top of the tallest tower of the castle to the south, the black sorcerer stood as if in a trance. The view from this spot would have been breathtaking, had it not been for the fact that the landscape around the tower had been destroyed by the Sorcerer's underground machinery, and the ogres. But the sorcerer did not come up here for the view. For him, it was simply the place where his magic would have the strongest effect, much as an antenna helps a radio transmitter to send its signals. With his eyes closed, he slowly rocked side to side, quietly reciting incantations intended to weave powerful spells of protection around him, and to retain control over his ogres. He was uneasy. For the first time in a thousand years, he had felt a magic pulse where there should not have been one. Someone had used an ogre stone.

And if that weren't enough, he had been told that some men had been sighted in his territory, and that some of his ogres had chased after them, to capture them. When he used his magic to see where they had gone, and what had transpired, there was a strange gray mist over everything, and he could not tell the outcome, or who had been involved. Although he did not know it, the Old Man of the Forest had used his own skills to cloud the sorcerer's vision, and keep him from learning the truth as long as possible.

The sorcerer suspected his brother, but as yet there was no evidence. What was going on? He had been sending ogres to kill The Old Man of the Forest for quite some time. For although he held him in the deepest contempt, he also knew that he held the key to ruining all of the plans that he had worked on for the past few thousand years. And the sorcerer had no intention of joining his people. He wanted to stay right where he was, and control every inch of this magical world.

"Blasted dull-witted beasts!" The sorcerer muttered, looking at the ogre who had been standing guard by the door quietly. It is true, ogres are not very smart, or dependable. He could never be sure if they did not return from his missions because they were destroyed, or because they found life on the other side of the mountains to be more interesting.

That is, until yesterday, when two returned with prisoners. Two ogres. Out of the dozens he had sent out. The sorcerer could not believe that his brother could deal with so many at once. No, he must have had help. But all that they brought back were a dwarf and a wolf.

He wondered if there were a clan of dwarves he did not know about. Perhaps the wolf was this dwarf's pet. It was time he found out just what was going on.

"Ogre, bring me the two prisoners that were brought in yesterday. It is time I forced them to tell me what they know." He said, and then added as an afterthought "And I want to see the ogres that brought them in, too."

The ogre nodded his big head and padded out of the room. The sorcerer shook his head. Dealing with his brother had been much more expensive than he'd ever expected. But surely, the fact that two ogres returned meant that they had finally succeeded. The Old Man would never have let them return with prisoners.

The ogre moved quietly for one so large. Down the staircase of the tower, through the dark damp halls and then even farther down, into chambers carved into the living rock of the mountainside itself. All that adorned the smooth walls were occasional torches, lighting the way. At the end of the passageway, which was now dripping with moisture, was a great door with two ogres standing before it. "Grom! We've not eaten for days! Have you come to relieve us?" one of them asked.

"Shut yer trap, Waxum! I've got an even better treat fer ya. Ye've been ordered to the tower, with the prisoners ye brought back."

"Argh!" moaned the ogre who so far had remained silent, "I hate goin' afore thet blasted Sorcerer! It usually means work!"

"Well, now! That'll teach ye to do yer job now, won't it Borg? If ye'd had sense to stay on the other side of the mountains like the rest, ye'd be eatin' yer fill of the local oxen by now!"

"I'm tellin' ye, our brethren ain't eatin' nothin' over there!" argued Borg. "There was dozens of 'em jest turned back to stone, and we two were attacked by hundreds of wolves! We were lucky to get out alive!"

"Right, and I'm a little pink dwarf!" laughed Grom. "Save them tall tales fer the sorcerer! But I warn ye, tellin' him thet yer whole force was wiped out by a bunch o' dogs won't go over big! He's likely to toss ye off the top o' the tower!"

"Bah! That job were doomed from the start! I hate ridin' that dragon! Ye hang on to whatever ye kin grab hold of, and hope the thing don't drop ye off fer a joke. And this time he sent so many of us, we had to wait fer hours while the dragon went back and forth carryin' us. They knew we were out and about long afore we were ready to move."

This conversation had gone on as the ogre Grom used great iron keys to unlock the door they had been guarding, and they entered the dungeon. A small dwarf and a large wolf, both still tightly bound, lay on the floor.

"By thunder, Waxum! Look at 'em. They be beat up bad! I hope they kin still talk, or ye might end up ground to dust one piece at a time by thet Sorcerer."

"Ah, they still got some life left in 'em." snarled Waxum. "And if it were you what barely made it back alive, you'd have been no less rough on 'em. They's responsible fer the death of over thirty of our brethren."

"There ye go agin' with them wild tales! Didn't I jest warn ye to drop that drivel?"

The voices faded, as the three ogres argued their way down the passageway back towards the castle dragging their captives, and the dungeon grew silent.

On the floor of the dungeon, was a metal square, which moved ever so slightly.

14 FINAL PREPARATIONS

King Ammon's army had moved as quickly as possible towards the sorcerer's castle. Occasionally their columns stumbled upon ogre patrols, so their scouts again were employed, this time to find the patrols and return to report their whereabouts, so the army could surround and attack them before they could escape and forewarn the sorcerer. He was certain to have learned from his spies that movement was afoot, but if they moved quickly enough, he would not be able to learn how strong a force approached, and he would not be able to prepare appropriate defenses or any traps.

King Ammon decided to keep the army traveling into the night to the edge of the forest where the plains below the Sorcerers' castle lay. Time was of the essence. Their attack must come the next day. Very little could be seen that night, as they moved ahead. Occasionally, the clinking of metal chains or the creaking of supply wagons was heard. From time to time, the heavy tread of King Ammon's secret weapons shook the stillness of the night, or the snap of thick tree branches might be heard when the trees of the forest were so thick that these huge weapons could barely fit between their trunks. There were men in the army who had never seen these weapons before, and their eyes widened in wonder. Surely, such a creature did not exist!

Outside the ruins of the dwarves' castle, Smarlog and his band watched the sun set in the west before sliding silently out of the gully and crawling on their stomachs from one grassy hummock to the next. Slowly, they made their way to the debris which now lay at the foot of the castle walls. All unnecessary equipment had been left in the gully. If they did not return tomorrow to retrieve it, it would be because they did not survive this task and therefore needed it no longer.

As Smarlog wormed his way through the grass, he thought he heard a rustle behind him. Since all the men had gone before him, and he had his pack in front of him, it could not have come from his band. "Too light for an ogre, too small for a dragon, who at any rate is inside. What could follow us?" he thought. Reaching a sandy spot where he could silently roll to the side, he did so, and drew his dagger. If some small spy for the sorcerer is nearby, it must never return.

Whatever it was, it was quite good at silent movement, for he could make out a shadow moving in the moonlight, but never heard another noise. When it came within reach of his hiding place, he recognized the shape as that of a dwarf! Tossing a pinch of sand at the shadow, it froze, turning its head slowly towards him. Seeing his low form in the depression, it made a small sign, which he recognized as a secret wave only known by the Smar clan, and he breathed a sigh of relief.

The two forms slid towards each other. Finally, close enough for each to be sure that the form in front of them was truly what it seemed, Smarlog and the other dwarf sheathed their daggers and held hands in greeting.

Afraid to speak here, where one noise could give away all, Smarlog went on, leading the way towards the wall where the rest of the band waited in silence, wondering what had taken the Smarlog so long. As his head appeared parting the grass where they sat flat up against the wall, he held his finger to his lips to encourage their silence, then waved in the other dwarf. The men's eyebrows raised in surprise, but no one spoke.

Feeling the wall, Smarlog could see that the disrepair caused by years of being ignored would make it easier to climb. There were many crevices where the masonry had crumbled, and thick vines protruded occasionally as well. One of the Purplemen tapped Smarlog on the shoulder, raised four fingers, and pointed up. Smarlog understood this to mean that four of the men had already begun the climb. He had hoped to be the first one up the wall, since he was lightest, but the four that chose to lead the climb were the younger Orangemen, and they were quite nimble.

Feeling for a grip, he was about to begin the climb himself, when he saw a rope slowly snake it's way down. Tying it around his waist, he started up. The four men above kept the rope taut, making him feel nearly weightless, but they did not attempt to haul him up, which might have dislodged a stone, making noise.

Smarlog could not help stopping for a moment halfway up, and looking out over the plain in the moonlight. With darkness, much of the scars across the land were invisible, and the silver moonlight gave the scene a surreal but clean look. It was very much like he remembered as a lad.

Once Smarlog was at the top, the rope was sent down again and the other dwarf raised, then the process repeated for the next person. By silent agreement, the heavier Purplemen had been left for last, since the chance of noise would be greatest raising them.

Once the two dwarves were on the parapet, they fell to preparing the contents of Smarlog's pack. Straight out of the pack, the bundle appeared to be a roll of fine threads. Treading softly towards the area where the roof had been smashed through by the dragon, they carefully unrolled the bundle. Now it could be seen that this was a net, made of incredibly fine strands. Strands no thicker than those found in a spider's web. By this time, all the Orangemen were up. Four men pulled up the inkeeper, while one of the original climbers came to aid the dwarves. Standing near the broken wall, the Orangeman could see some light and smoke escaping from the huge hole. He held his long spear at the ready, in case the dragon heard a noise and came to investigate. It was unlikely that he could do much but slow the inevitable, but perhaps he could partially blind the creature, making it possible for future freedom fighters to win their battle.

The net was now nearly ready to anchor to one side of the hole, and they found suitable debris such as chunks of charred timbers and broken wall stones, which they slid into carefully designed pockets along the edges of the net. The eastern sky seemed to be slightly silver, now. The first Purpleman made his way silently over the wall's edge, and took over the lifting from two Orangemen, who now rested from the duty. Once they felt their muscles stop trembling so they could trust them again, they went to assist in filling the pockets of the net with debris. As each pocket was filled, the net was stretched a bit further around the hole, and the process would begin again. The last Purpleman clambered onto the roof as an orange glow brightened the eastern line where the sky and land met. They were only halfway done but now, with more men, the process went quicker. And by the time the shapes of the band on the roof could be seen clearly, the net was almost fully in place. There was no darkness left to hide in. From time to time, the men looked over at the strange new dwarf. This one wasn't dressed for travel. He looked to be ready to fight.

Away south, with the brightening of the day, the lookouts on the Sorcerer's castle could tell that something was different about the forest edging the northeast plain. There had been some obvious indications even earlier in the way of noises. Something large approached the plain. But now with the coming of light, something else began to show from time to time. There was a glint of something shiny reflecting the early morning sky. The ogres looked at each other. Dull-witted as they could be, they knew warfare, and the sign of an approaching army. A messenger was sent to inform the Sorcerer. The ogre chosen was not happy to be the one. The Sorcerer did not always take bad news well.

In the dark shadows within the woods, Numbers One through Twelve approached King Ammon and The Old Man of the Forest, who stood with their generals, consulting maps laid over a fallen tree.

"Beggin' yer pardon, sirs. But we've been thinking, and well, frankly, sir, we're not the soldierly type, ye see?"

King Ammon, thinking that they wished to be relieved of any responsibility, said graciously "Oh, of course. You gentlemen have been of great help to now. If you'd like to retire, we..."

Number Ones eyes widened, and he interrupted the king. "Oh, no Sar! Nothin' like thet! It's jest that we don't think we'd be best used to step out here where these here fella's are about to do what they'd been trained to do, and after all, we've come to see what we kin do about this here cloud thet's been such a pain in everyone's side. So, we thought we'd ask ter be allowed ter swing around this here plain ter the left. We've noticed a grayness there, and either the cloud is a'comin' agin, or we don't know beans!"

"Eh?" Looking over to where the farmer pointed, a series of gray plumes could now be seen to be rising up from the hills below and southeast of the castle. "By thunder, you're right! Looking at the Old Man of the Forest, who smiled and shrugged his shoulders, the king said "Sergeant at Arms! Make sure these warriors are provided with anything they feel they may need to plug those cursed holes!"

"Yes Sir!" saluted the Sergeant. "Men! Follow me!"

And the farmers were led off to the store of weapons.

In the depths of the castle, the metal grate had finally quietly broken free. With a long heave, Christopher and Smartwig pushed it far enough over to the side to allow them to clamber into the dungeon. Sitting on the floor next to the hole, they caught their breath. Moving the grate had taken all of their strength.

"Let's rest." suggested Christopher.

Smartwig nodded.

Suddenly both of them froze. "Did you hear that?" Smartwig asked.

"From down there?" Christopher replied.

Smartwig nodded.

"I'm all rested. Aren't you?" Christopher asked.

In answer, Smartwig began sliding the grate back over the hole. He was taking too long for Christopher, who ran over to help speed things up. Once it was in place, they bolted for the door.

But the ogres had locked the door again on the way out. Even with both their shoulders against it, it didn't budge.

15 INTO BATTLE

Number One now led the way through hundred-foot piles of rank steaming ash and soot. The band of farmers, all armed with nine pound sledge hammers, filed along, looking every which way for ogres, and a reason for this mess.

Finally, they passed a series of round vents in the ground, thirty feet across, from which a grayish-brown smoke had begun to pour in earnest.

"The cloud?" asked Number Eleven.

"Likely." nodded Number One grimly. "And it looks like 'himself' is gearin' up ter' ruin somebody's day agin. Whaddya say we change thet?"

The band grinned. "It's about time we got our two cents in, thets' what I think." said Number Seven, waving his hammer.

As they rounded what must have been the hundredth mountain of greasy soot, they came upon a good size shed. "Maybe there's somethin' in there we kin larn from." Number One said. "Foller me."

Sneaking up on the building, they peered into the open door. There was a set of stairs in the center of the shed. The pulsing of machinery could be heard coming up from deep down in the earth.

"Well, we ain't got nowhar te go but down, I guess." said Number One. And he began to trot down the stairs. Without hesitation, his eleven companions followed.

The Sorcerer was already in a foul mood when the ogre strode in to break the news of the approaching army. He had only just begun to question the captive dwarf, when a spy in the form of a shaggy black bird had come to the window to give him a full briefing on the outcome of the battle of the Forty Ogre Woods. He was nearly foaming at the mouth in irritation, and the ogre reporting the new army nearly at their doorstep received a stroke across the forehead with a nearby broom for his troubles.

"Get the guard out to the plain!" he shrieked. "I want that army destroyed before one soldier lays a hand on our castle wall! I cannot be challenged this way! I won't have it!"

In his anger, he chased all the ogres in the chamber down the stairs and out of the tower, before he remembered the captives, still bound up and awaiting further questioning.

The ogres ran out to sound the march, while the Sorcerer raced back up the tower stairs. Battle horns sounded from the towers, and ogres now poured out the gates, to line up for battle. This time, the men would face not forty surprised ogres, but thousands, ready and as angry as demons.

Quickly, they formed ranks, and began the long trek across the plain towards the forest.

But now from the trees came answering trumpeting. Trumpeting not only from the battle horns of the king's army, but from huge gray beasts that not only rivaled, but surpassed the great size of the ogres. Hundreds of beasts that now strode out of the forest with their keepers beside them.

King Ammon, in the center of his line of troops with The Old Man of the Forest, looked at the oncoming ogres, and then at his line of attacking troops. The elephants were definitely going to come in handy. But even with this secret weapon, he could see the day would not go well. "We've not enough men, Old Man. We'll make a good show, but we cannot turn the tide with these forces."

The front lines of King Ammon's army had now broken out of the trees, when suddenly, gray fur covered shapes streaked past the rear of the army to catch up with the first line of elephants. Hundreds of huge snarling wolves, preparing to cause what havoc they could as the armies met.

For a moment, the two armies stopped, perhaps a hundred feet from each other. Then there was a great shout, and the lines rushed towards each other. Even with the confusion and roar of battle, King Ammon could see a hoard of purple and dull orange shapes rush out of the forest to the south, towards the melee. Fearing that his scouts had failed, and his army was now to be trapped in a flanking attack, he was about to shout a retreat to the trees when he saw the hoard converge not on his troops, but on the flank of the ogres.

"Who are they?" He shouted to The Old Man of the Forest.

"Friends of the dwarves, I'll wager." responded the Old Man.

"And where are the dwarves?" asked King Ammon, as he raised his battleaxe and charged towards a nearby ogre.

In response, the Old Man pointed towards the north, where hundreds of dwarves now rounded the foothills of the mountains on which sat the Sorcerer's castle, with their banners unfurled. Their battle cries could not be heard from this distance but their open mouths could be plainly seen.

Still trapped in the dungeon, Christopher and Smartwig stood with their backs to the door and their swords in their hands as the metal grate opened for the second time in a thousand years. Looking at each other, they nodded.

"Been good knowin' ye, Christopher."

"You too." Christopher said in a wavery voice.

Then a head of black hair popped up from the hole in the floor. It was the head of a man, who looked more than a little surprised by the two small souls who now expected to lose their lives before him. "By thunder! Little people!" And his head dropped down out of sight.

"Come here! Quick! I'm telling you the truth!" They could hear him shout.

Now two shaggy heads with wide eyes popped up, and then down out of sight again.

Finally, one entire man climbed up and out of the hole, with his hands empty and open, his sword sheathed. "Be you from the Smar Clan?"

Smartwig said in a guarded voice, "I be."

"Then We've met yer kin, jest north o' here not more'n a day ago! They're on their way to storm the gate, they said! Thet's why we came! We've been living in the mountains to the west o' here fightin' off ogres since I don't remember when, and figgered we'd take advantage o' what we larned over the years to help 'em out."

"We?" asked Christopher.

In answer, a dozen men, definitely warriors, now popped out of the hole. There's a sight more still climbin'." The first one said.

Smartwig, now terribly outnumbered, and a bit in awe of the men who seemed not to care about whether their presence was noticed by the ogres, managed to stammer out that they might not get much farther than this anyway, since the great oak door was locked.

"Is that a fact? Maybe Tiny can fix that." responded the spokesman.

"Who's Tiny?" asked Christopher.

"Hey, Tiny! Come on up front, 'ere." The man shouted down the hole.

After some scuffling below, a new head appeared. A rather good sized head. An impressively large head, in fact. His shoulders would not fit through the yard wide hole, and he had to duck back down and put his arms through first to fit.

He unwedged himself and strode to the front. He was nearly as large as an ogre.

"This gen'lman 'ere says this door is stuck." Said the spokesman.

Tiny nodded, and looked angrily at the door. Christopher stepped back, pulling Smartwig with him.

74

Tiny crouched down, and stuffed his huge fingers into the crack underneath the door. Next, putting his shoulder to the door, he grunted, pulled, and leaned, all at once. With a cracking of timber, the door shattered, and Tiny fell on the remains, as the men behind whooped and ran over him as if he were a bridge over a stream. Once the line of men had stormed off down the hallway into the castle in search of someone to do battle with, Tiny got up and lumbered off after them.

The Sorcerer had run back to his chamber, and looked out the window over the plain. He was about to gloat to the dwarf and his pet about the destruction of the raiding army when he noticed the elephants. Studying the field more closely, he realized that the ogres were losing ground. With a yelp, he ran to a large red gem mounted in a brass tripod, and waving his hands over the gem began speaking dark incantations. Stopping briefly, he looked at the dwarf and snarled "Let's see how your friends fare against the dragon!"

Smarstick and the Prince of wolves had been madly loosening their bonds for hours, whenever no one was looking directly at them. Now, the Prince of Wolves had managed to get some of the rope binding his mouth shut inside of his mouth, and his razor sharp teeth made short work of it.

But just then, three ogres ran in to tell the Sorcerer that the remains of the guard was now battling their way back to the castle, and some of the local mountain men had somehow made their way into the castle and were fighting inside.

"Make ready my bird on the roof, in case I need to escape this madness!" He ordered.

One ogre ran off up the stairs to do his bidding.

"Ah ha! The spell is done, the dragon is called!" The Sorcerer shouted.

Turning to the ogres, the Sorcerer seemed to regain some composure.

"Tell the guard to leave the field and defend from the walls. Let the dragon finish off the attackers."

"And do something about those mountain men!"

16 SUMMON THE DRAGON

The Sorcerer's summons came to a dragon already awakened.

Down in the great hall of the castle where the dragon slept, strange but familiar odors had warned the beast that something was afoot. His first reaction was to make sure that the treasures he had gathered here were safe. Nothing had been moved, and his steel-gray eyes roved the darkened walls, looking for clues. There were times that unsuspecting mortals drifted past the castle, and made for tasty snacks. Perhaps this was simply one of those times. In just a few moments more, if he had not been called by the sorcerer, he would have left his lair to investigate anyway.

But inside his head, he could hear the summoning voice of The Master, and he must obey. Vaulting up he spread his wings, but only partially, since even here in the great hall there was not enough room for him to extend them to their full length. Not until he was clear of the castle.

Still, he had enough room to launch himself into the air, and with a few swings of his massive wings, soared upwards toward the hole of light at the highest part of the hall roof. As he neared the exit, he noticed the iridescent glow from the strands of the net, now completely across the entrance. But he thought little of it. What could spider threads do to a dragon? Smarlog stood at the edge of the hole, as the dragon's huge horned head appeared. So large, it took a full second for the entire head to pass on it's upward climb. The threads stretched and started to hum as the beast ran into the net. The pockets of debris began to twist and slide towards the opening. "Grab the weights, they can't be allowed to move yet!" yelled Smarlog, diving on the nearest one. The troop followed suit. As if in slow motion, the men watched the tremendous beast as it glided past them, so close they could nearly touch the huge scales.

Now the monster's shoulders and wings broke past the hole, and he spread his wings to their full size to propel him even higher. Seeing the tiny little creatures on his roof, he was furious. How dare they come so close? Stroking his wings back for elevation, the rest of his body now shot out of the hole, angling up and away from the castle. The little men below struggled to hold the weighted pockets in place. He was a hundred feet up now, and his wings fully back, ready to reopen. He could feel the pressure of the tiny little strands on him now, even through his protective scales, and he decided that the Sorcerer must wait. These foolish mortals must die first.

But when he tried to bring his wings forward for a second stroke, he found that he could not, and the ground rushed up to meet him with amazing speed. On the roof, the web now hummed as loudly as a harp, with the tension of the dragon and the wind through the threads, and the men could no longer hold the weights in place. They soared in an arc after the dragon, twirling around each other and entrapping the dragon completely. The men stood amazed, watching the dragon now rocketing towards the ground, head first.

With a thunderous crash, the beast met the earth, forming a huge crater from which it bounced over backwards only to crash down again, this time sliding to a stop near the gully where the men had spent the day before. Even at a distance, they could hear groaning and creaking of the machinery of the dragon as the net did its work, draining the magic from the beast and constricting about the remains like an anaconda. Before their eyes, the beast slowly began to grow smaller.

Smarlog, being the leader he was, had begun to collect himself already. Dusting his hands off, he said "Well, looks like we'd best get an oxcart out thet way, to clear up the mess." as if trapping dragons in spiderwebs was something one did every day.

The men looked at each other in wonder.

"I'd not had the opportunity last night to properly introduce Smarbark here." Smarlog went on. "Where be the rest o' the army, Smarbark?"

Still looking over at the remains of the beast that moments ago could have turned them all to ash, Smarbark said "Army? Oh, yes, of course. Well, they were headed for the Sorcerers castle. Would you believe it? We were visited by a talking wolf! He told us that two armies were converging on the mountain. We went to help."

"Oh, I believe it." Smarlog replied.

There was a brief burst of flame and smoke from the dragon.

In the tower of the Sorcerer, things had heated up to such a point that it seemed prudent for the Sorcerer to begin moving important magical artifacts to the roof where his magical bird sat ready to carry him to safety. Ignoring Smarstick and the Prince of Wolves, whom he thought were sufficiently tied, he kept bounding up and down the stairs with amulets and mysterious devices adding them to a pack on the back of a giant black condor.

Reentering his magic chamber, he was gathering his last armful of possessions when the door flew open, and Christopher and Smartwig ran in, closely pursued by two ogres.

The sight of the sorcerer stopped them in their tracks, and they were scooped up by their pursuers, wiggling and yelling.

"What's this? Dwarves? No! One dwarf, and one man-boy! Do you mean to tell me your army is being beaten by children now, Grom?" shouted the sorcerer. Grom, distracted by the sorcerers insult, held Christopher up to his face for closer inspection. In response, Christopher swung his head forward, bashing into Grom's nose with all his might.

"Ow!" the ogre shouted, startled, dropping Christopher, who landed on a table of glass instruments, with a crash.

In the ensuing confusion, Smarstick and the Prince of Wolves broke their remaining bonds. Smarstick began throwing whatever loose articles he could find at the two ogres' heads. The Prince of Wolves, although weak from the ordeal, threw himself at the ogre still carrying Smartwig. The ogre used Smartwig as a bat, holding him by the feet to swat the wolf back. The Sorcerer backed towards the stairs to the tower roof, then spun and ran.

"He has a means of escape up there!" shouted Smarstick.

"Stop him!" shouted Smartwig to Christopher. Then, even as he was being swung about the room like a badminton racket he added, "We'll take care of these two!"

Christopher knew what Smartwig was thinking. The Sorcerer would be stopped by someone not of this world. Somehow, up to this point, Christopher had not thought much about what he could do or how he could do it. But he had always expected to have a lot of backing when the time came. But now here he was, the only one in a position to even confront the Sorcerer. And he still had no clue as to how he could stop him.

But up the stairs he went, because if he didn't, he and his friends would probably meet their end in this room anyway.

The Sorcerer had been up and down the stairs so many times this day that his energy was spent. Christopher was nearly able to catch up with him in the stairwell. He caught sight of the Sorcerer as he ducked out the door to the roof. Bursting out onto the roof himself, he saw the Sorcerer tossing the last of his load carelessly into the pack, and clambering onto the back of the huge bird.

"Not so fast, bucko!" shouted Christopher, who couldn't think of what else to do.

Turning, the sorcerer's face went from worry to amusement when he saw the small being before him. "Bah!" he said, and waving his hand in a magic sign, he launched a spell at Christopher who was immediately surrounded by a brief blast of smoke and flames.

But only momentarily, and it blew away in the wind. "Could this be what they meant?" he thought. "Perhaps his magic has little effect on someone from another world."

Realizing that he still carried his bag of magic marbles, he fumbled in his robe for them as he shouted at the sorcerer again "Is that the best you can do?"

Astounded, the sorcerer stopped in his tracks. He had assumed the little boy would be blown off the roof. "What, then? You are not of my people, but any boy of this world should have been ashes! Perhaps my aim is off today. Very well, then, I'll be more careful, and use a stronger spell!"

While Christopher had not been as damaged by the last spell as expected, it didn't seem a good idea to just stand around and let a sorcerer take pot shots at him so he ducked behind the stairwell entrance. This time the effect of the spell was stronger, and bits of stone were even chipped off the parapet where Christopher had stood.

Christopher had found his magic marbles and he threw one of the eight at the ground in front of the sorcerer. As usual, the objects were totally unpredictable, and a huge tree appeared where the marble fell. The sorcerer was surprised but obviously not injured, and now becoming irritated. He decided to teach this foolish boy a lesson. Stepping around the tree, he began to wave his hands again, when a small barn owl flew in front of his face, slashing at his eyes with it talons. He released his spell as he ducked, ruining his aim, and his spell shot harmlessly off into the air.

Christopher now threw all seven of his remaining marbles in desperation at the feet of the sorcerer. "Oh, please, please, be something useful!" he thought.

The marbles bounced, and rolled all about the roof. When they stopped, there were seven puffs of smoke, and seven more Christophers appeared. They all dashed at Christopher and then ran around him in different directions. He found he needed to jump and dodge them to prevent collisions. The sorcerer quickly became completely confused as to which one was the real Christopher.

Rolling up his sleeves, he began the process of elimination, blasting at each Christopher spell after blinding hot spell. Now there were seven christophers, then six, then five, four, three...

Down the stairwell, could be heard a familiar voice thundering seven magic words, and then silence, as two ogres slowly turned to stone.

The sorcerer's eyes widened. "My brother?" he gasped, and abandoned his plan to destroy Christopher. He turned once again to climb aboard the condor and escape. The last Christopher standing grabbed hold of the skirt of the sorcerer's robe and ran in the other direction in an attempt to delay him just a bit longer. It worked momentarily, but the sorcerer slipped his arms out of the robe, caught his balance, and turned back to his feathered beast.

17 FROM TUNNELS TO TOWERS

Number One had led his band of intrepid farmers-turned-warriors deep into the earth. Following their ears toward the sounds of the machinery they felt surely must be causing the cloud. They ran down dark passages, ducking behind timbers or anything at hand when they encountered ogres. Some seemed to be hauling material to be burned in the great machines the sorcerer had designed for some dark purpose or another. The great engines pulsed and smoked, glowed and spun, and their thundering shook the men to their core the closer they approached the cavern where they lay. The smell of sulfur was so strong in the air that their eyes streamed with tears. Finally they entered the great chamber where the powerful throbbing engines stood in row after row, driving great pistons that turned gears and wheels and chains and driveshafts in a confusing, overpowering concert of deafening machine-made sound. Deciding that stopping these machines dead in their tracks would probably do some dandy damage, Number One motioned over his shoulder at his followers, and charged down the stairs into the center of the clockwork of huge gears, before any ogres could stop them.

Once there, each farmer selected a spot of their own, and jammed their sledge hammers deep into the gears. Immediately, there began a grinding noise, and the heads of all ogres in the chamber spun to the center, where the farmers now stood. The gears still moved, but there were groans and great sounds of rending metal, and the teeth of gears began to strip off, chains began to snap, driveshafts to bend and twist, gears became misshapen and deadly pieces of metal began to fly through the air.

The thought that perhaps this might not be the safest place for a farmer to be under the circumstances, seemed to occur to all twelve of the band at once. Each man began to seek his own way through the twisted metal and whirling deadly parts (not to mention raging ogres,) in an attempt to reach

81

the stairs out of the chamber.

However, due to the position of most of the ogres at the time that the farmers were discovered, the best they could do was duck and dodge swinging arms and kicking feet, crawling on their hands and knees into holes in the machinery where ogres could not fit, and sometimes even running between the legs of the ogres themselves, until they finally all had collected at a side door to the great chamber. They all ducked through the door whooping and nyuk-nyuking and, to be quite frank, having a much better time than one would have imagined under the circumstances. Perhaps it was some sort of a relief to be able to strike back after all these years that gave them such a feeling of happiness as they ran.

But the ogres were not far behind, and gaining, even though the farmers continued to dodge into whatever smaller sub-shafts and tunnels they could find. Running past one door, however, Number One skidded to a halt. He could hear yet another engine running and he was not about to leave any machinery intact if at all possible. So the band narrowly missed capture by running back at the door, and crashing through it past two startled ogres.

They found themselves in a lesser chamber with a pit directly in front of them filled with black oily water. Apparently, the engine they heard was a pump that prevented the flooding of the underground labyrinth that they had been traversing. The band ran to the opposite wall of the chamber where a round wooden form about ten feet across was wedged into a hole. The wooden form was held in place by several large timbers propped against it, and water trickled out from between it and the rock wall. The only other exit was now blocked by dozens of angry ogres.

Grabbing up some spare pieces of timber littering the floor, the farmers desperately began smashing the braces in hopes of escaping by forcing this blockage open and dashing out the hole.

The ogres now had looks of horror on their faces, and ran at them shouting "Plug! Plug!"

What the ogres meant became immediately clear, as there was a crack of fracturing wood, and the large wooden form suddenly leaped out of place, driven by the river of water which it had been holding back. Sweeping the twelve farmers before it, the big round plug was thrown across the chamber, and the whole collection slammed into the ogres. They, in turn, were catapulted backwards into the wall around the entrance, smashing the walls away and enlarging the hole so that the plug, complete with farmers, was now swept out into the shaft and back along the passageway.

The raging torrent of water, of course, rushed into every available crevice, passageway, and chamber. In a matter of a few minutes, it filled even the great chamber, and drowned all the ogres trapped underground.

Clinging desperately to the wooden form, the twelve stunned farmers now were being rushed along a dark sooty passageway like a bullet down a barrel, awaiting their doom at the end of the tunnel. Their shouts could not be heard above the roar of the water, and the light was dim, giving the entire event a frightful aspect.

They could see a somewhat brighter light at the end of the tunnel they were now rocketing down, and awaited some fate such as being crushed against a stone wall, or drowned in the dark, greasy, acrid water hundreds of feet below the surface of the earth.

But suddenly the tunnel curved upwards, and the wooden form slipped from an upright position to a horizontal one, scooping up the twelve forms clinging desperately to the plug in hopes of a lucky break. They were covered with the stinking black soot from head to toe, and all that could be seen of them was the whites of their eyes now, as large around as they could ever be. Onward the wooden plug rushed, and upward the tunnel curved, until they recognized the very spiral stairs down which they had so recently boldly trotted.

Above ground, on the battlefield, nearly all of the ogres had retreated back into the castle, and the plains had quieted greatly. Suddenly, where moments before the ash pits to the south west had been spewing a stinking brown-black cloud, there was a deep rumbling as if a volcano were about to erupt, and the plumes turned to gray, then white, as if they had become steam vents. The rumbling went on for three or four minutes, and the men could feel the ground shake all around them. Ogre and man alike briefly stopped their fighting, to see what was happening in the ash pits.

Suddenly, there was a loud popping noise, and what appeared to be a small shed went sailing through the air, tumbling end over end. Next came a strange gurgling noise, and then a column of water rose up close to two hundred feet in the air. Even more curious, there appeared to be a dozen or so men standing on the top of the column of water, dancing.

Slowly, the column of water subsided, and the dancing men were gently lowered back down, out of sight behind the piles of ash and soot.

Realizing that they had stopped fighting, both sides now took to each other with renewed vigor.

By now the armies were at the walls of the Sorcerers castle, battering the gate in earnest. Behind them lay the remains of friend and foe alike, a tribute to the ferocity of the battle. The wolves stepped back to regroup and prepare for the final assault, since men and dwarves are better suited to attacking walls than four footed creatures of the forest. Throwing up ladders, and charging the door with battering rams, the men repeatedly were repulsed by the ogres on the walls. It looked like a stalemate might be in the making.

But the mountain men who had snuck inside through the same route as Christopher and Smartwig were finally able to work their way to the breastworks and confound the defending ogres from their own heights, allowing enough attackers to scale the walls and force the remaining ogres to retreat to their next line of defense. Several of the mountain men ran to the gate and after a brief and ferocious fight with some ogres, managed to lift the huge oaken bar that held the gates closed. A column of dwarves with battleaxes wasted no time in entering the gate and pressing the defending ogres back within the walls.

The sound of battle grew even louder, and could be heard clearly on the roof of the Sorcerers tower, where the sorcerer had been once again preparing to mount his condor. But two battered and tired but determined forms beat him to the big bird – a dwarf and a wolf. Leaping atop the condor's back themselves, the sight of the wolf startled the bird into spreading its wings and stepping off the roof. It spiraled down towards the courtyard below, with the dwarf trying madly to learn how to guide the creature before they struck something or worse, landed in the midst of the angry ogres clustering in a defensive manner at the courtyard walls.

Insane with rage now, the sorcerer turned back to the remaining three Christophers. "You! Whatever, whoever you are, you have ruined everything!" he shouted, and began a horrifying incantation that would rip asunder the entire rooftop. Two of the Christophers now faded away, the magic of the marbles losing strength, and the real Christopher was left behind to face the sorcerer alone.

Alone, that is, except for one last figure who now stepped through the stairwell door. The Old Man of the Forest shouted "Enough!" and began to cast his own spells at the sorcerer.

There now began a magical duel of legendary proportions, and many below thought that a passing thunderstorm must have surrounded the tower, for it was hidden from view in a black and silver swirling cloud, while lighting crackled and roared from the heights in every direction.

"Get below and help your friend Smartwig escape the tower!" shouted the Old Man. "He is already on his way down the stairs. You have no time to lose!"

Christopher dashed across the rooftop to the doorway without further encouragement. As he reached the door, he heard the Old Man shout again.

"Christopher!"

Turning, Christopher could see that the two were standing only a few feet away from each other, with lightning bolts crashing so close around them that their robes were smoking.

Over the crashing thunder, he could not hear the final words of the Old Man, but it looked like he simply shouted "Thank you!"

Christopher felt like he was abandoning his ally this way, but as he watched, the two were now totally enveloped in blinding sheets of crackling electricity, and to approach them was completely impossible.

Dashing down the steps two at a time, through the chamber, past two granite statues that had not been there previously, and on down towards the great hall he ran. Soon he came upon a small shape limping slowly down the stairs. Jumping in front of Smartwig (for of course, that was who it was,) he leaned backward and the nearly unconscious dwarf simply collapsed forward onto Christopher's shoulders. Burdened with the extra weight, but spurred on by the roaring winds and thunder from up above that seemed to continue to grow ever louder and more intense, Christopher somehow continued to plod down the stairs with his friend draped on his back.

The walls and stairs were shaking and cracking, and bits of masonry pelted him from above as he made it down the last turn to the door. Reaching out and lifting the latch, he pushed the door open and staggered into the courtyard. There, in the center of the courtyard was the condor, lying on the ground, obviously injured. Smarstick was unable to steer the frightened bird, and it must have hit one of the defending walls while spiraling down. He and the Prince of Wolves now stood by the bird's body, ducking blows by several ogres who had witnessed their crash-landing. Noticing Christopher stagger towards them, the ogres stopped to watch him carry his burden and lay the now limp dwarf by his other two friends, then turn to pull his sword to help defend them to the end.

Suddenly there was another great crack, and looking up, they all watched as the top half of the tower leaned out over them, separated from the base, and hurtled down to crush them all.

The ogres turned and ran, but the four allies were too exhausted, and watched the tower grow as it rushed to the ground.

Only moments before they were crushed to bits, the tower disappeared in a blinding white light, and when their sight returned a second later, they were showered not with tons of debris, but with a fine dust, as fine as flour. The tower had disappeared, and the Old Man and the Sorcerer had passed over to wherever the others of their ancient race had gone.

Christopher watched as the ogres who had run away now began to return to finish off the job they had begun. As they neared he leaped forward to defend as best he could, but he was one small human, and they were many and large, and he knew that this gesture would only bring the end faster. The first ogre to reach him raised his club over his head, but then suddenly bore a look of complete surprise, and toppled forward on top of Christopher.

18 THE AFTERMATH

When Christopher awoke, he was in a bed, in a stone room lined with beds just like his, and full of bodies of all sizes with bandages all over them, just like his. The scene was quite odd, because some of the bodies were quite large, with legs protruding over the ends of the beds as if the beds had been made for much smaller people. Some of the bodies had four legs and fur, and their legs protruded out the sides of the beds. And some of the littler bodies, although no bigger than boys, bore gray frazzled beards.

Christopher wondered whether he might be dreaming, or have simply lost his marbles. But the thought of marbles brought the whole frightening thing back and he suddenly tried to sit up in a panic.

This turned out to be a mistake, because he was quite bruised from the impact of the collapsing ogre.

"Owwwwwww!" His moan alerted a small nurse that he had regained consciousness, and she quickly stepped over to calm him down.

"Set right there, now, soldier, and let things mend some!" She said.

"Ohhh! Where am I? What happened? Did we win? How did I get here? Where is Smarstick and Smartwig and the Prince of Wolves? Are they alright?"

"So many questions!" tutted the nurse. "Ye'll find enough answers soon enough, young man! Meanwhile, rest. I'll fetch the doctor, he'll be wantin' to see how yer doin'."

A voice from the bed next to his now spoke. "Wal I kin answer some o' them questions, anyways. We're as right as ye kin git when ye been swatted about by ogres, anyways."

Christopher was so sore, he found it hard to roll over. "Smartwig?"

Finally, he was able to turn far enough to see the small dwarf in the bed next to his. His head was all bandaged up, his exposed face was purple and bruised, and his grin was missing a few teeth.

"Am I glad to see you!" said Christopher. "What happened?"

"Wal, to tell ye the truth it's all pretty blurry to me too! All I remember is ye carryin' me outta the tower. An' Smarstick an' the Prince o' Wolves said the condor crash is all they remember. Wolves! I guess they ain't too fond o' flyin.'"

"We most definitely are not!" said a form under a blanket in a bed across the row of beds from Christopher.

"Wow, are we all here then? Where's Smarstick?" said Christopher.

An arm in a cast rose from the bed next to the Prince of Wolves and a weak voice said "Present an' accounted fer, sar."

"Well I'd sure like to know the story." said Christopher. "The last thing I remember is an ogre coming down on me like a ton of … Hey! The tower! I remember that dropping, too!"

At this point, the doctor arrived to poke and prod at Christopher, test his reflexes, and check his vision. Behind him came Smarlog and King Ammon, and three men which Christopher did not recognize. They were introduced as the leaders of the Purple, Orange, and Mountain clans which had been so crucial in turning the tide of the battle. While the doctor examined him, King Ammon introduced himself and filled in some of the blanks. The room grew silent as he narrated the final moments of the ogre's defense.

"I was nearing the courtyard when the tower fell, but I had not gotten there yet. The defense of the ogres was vicious, and they fought to the very last. If the mountain men hadn't somehow found a way in, we would surely have lost many more men, and perhaps never have been able to storm the walls."

"As I turned the last passageway to the courtyard, the walls were still defended, but perhaps half of the ogres were looking inwards, rather than out, as if amazing things were happening within. It was quite a sight outside the walls too, I must say. I've never seen such a collection of armed creatures in my life! We had decided that the elephants would not be as effective in the confines of the castle passages, so it was up to the troops to finish the job by that time. There were the mountain men in leather and steel, and the men of the other neighboring lands, in their dull orange and purple robes sporting sledgehammers, my troops in chainmail and helmets, hundreds of wolves, and dwarves with battleaxes!"

"But we might be there still, if it wasn't for one man in a light gray robe, who managed to make his way to the wall while dodging all the huge blocks of stone that the ogres were now tossing down at us. He had collected a group of the mountain men around him, but it was plain he wasn't one of them. As a matter of fact, he didn't really look or act like a soldier. He just looked like getting inside that courtyard was the most important thing in the world. He strung some sort of rope or something in a big circle on the wall. I remember that there was a small black box the cord came out of. The men were so close to the wall that the ogres couldn't see them anymore. The rope must have been spun from some amazing special magic. Or maybe it was contained in the box, for once it was in place, he touched the box on some colorful spots adorning the front, and the surface of the wall inside the rope loop glowed a brilliant beautiful blue."

Christopher's heart began to race. Unwittingly, King Ammon had been describing a portable time-door. He waited, his hands shaking, to hear the rest.

"Then through the blue, we could see inside the courtyard! Imagine! Right through the wall! As soon as that happened, the man in the gray robe dashed inside. For a moment, no one could get up the nerve to follow. Funny, isn't it? Here we are, willing to stand and fight giants that were made from magic and stone, but we were afraid to walk through a hole!" But finally, one man worked up the nerve. I will never forget him, he was nearly as big as the ogres! Well, he scooped up three men, shouted a fierce yell, and ran after that gray magician, or whatever he was. Christopher, are you all right?"

Christopher nodded his head. Tears fell from his eyes. It had to be his father. But he had run, alone, right into the last stronghold of ogres. What were his chances?

King Ammon, watching Christopher with concern, continued his story. "The mountain men streamed into the hole with a battle cry once they saw their huge kinsman brave it. And we followed. By thunder! What a confusing battle that was! The last of the ogre's defenses were breached, and they fought like the demons they are! There were times we weren't standing on the ground, the fallen were so thick. Ours and theirs. But I remember seeing that huge fellow. He had just forced his way through the line of defending ogres in a mad rush. Why, he even picked up one ogre and swung him around like a club, as big as they are. Then four ogres turned on him, and dozens of our men were piling on top of those."

"And the man? The man in the gray robe?" asked Christopher, his voice quivering.

"I'm afraid I lost sight of him once he dashed through the hole. I'm not sure." King Ammon said.

"I know some." Came a deep voice from a corner of the ward. All heads turned, to see who spoke.

There in the corner were four beds all moved together to make one huge platform. On top of that was the massive form of a man that now sat up and swung his feet over onto the floor. So big was the man that sitting on the edge of the bed, his knees stuck up in the air.

"Tiny!" Christopher said.

The giant smiled. Then, in a deep booming voice, he said, "I saw him. Tried to follow. He ran to a fight in the middle of the courtyard. He ran up the back of an ogre, with a little dagger. Grabbed the ogre's hair. I couldn't see where the dagger went in, but the ogre went down like a tree. The other ogres leapt on him, then our men on them. Then more ogres on us. After that I don't know."

"Are all the wounded here?" asked Christopher. "I need to search the wards!"

The nurse began to argue, saying that he had broken ribs and needed to rest. Smarlog, seeing the look on his face, said "I'll arrange a search fer this man. Ye kin hardly sit up, let alone wander around. There's quite a few rooms like this, them ogres were a hardy bunch. They took a big toll."

At that very moment a man wrapped head to toe in bandages entered the ward on crutches. "Excuse me, I'm looking for a boy named Christopher. I'm his father." He announced to the room.

Behind him, twelve filthy but smiling farmers now appeared, covered in a stinking sulfurous soot. They shuffled into the room, and stood looking around at all the men and animals, who sat staring back at the odd sight.

"You smell terrible!" The man on the crutches said.

19 FAMILY TIME

"How did you find me? How did you know when I was?"

Christopher had been dying to ask that question since reunited with his father. But they were never alone, with all the merry making that went on in the castle once it became clear that the Sorcerer had been taken by The Old Man of the Forest, the dragon was now just a pile of spare parts in a very nice net bag, and the few ogres that escaped the battle were found and accounted for.

"You told me." said his father smiling.

"Me? How?" Christopher asked.

"The falcon head." he replied. "Let me start at the beginning. First, it quickly became clear that you didn't end up here when we expected you to be. The explosion had a somewhat predictable effect, so a little math told me the time range that we could expect you to be found in was only a few thousand years. At the most, maybe as many as eight thousand but the odds of that were thin."

"Oh, great, so all I had to do was live to be eight thousand years old and we would have met up anyway." Christopher said.

"Well, yes, that would work too. But rather than wait that long, we went to the earliest possible time, and looked around. We met a very interesting man. I sort of ran into him, you might say. I was in a bit of a hurry at the time, and couldn't stop to talk."

"Your father's trying to tell you he was chased by a sabre toothed tiger." interrupted Christopher's mother, who sat at the table of their cottage enjoying a cup of chamomile tea.

"That was you? He was right? Wow! That guy really was ancient!" Christopher said, amazed.

"Quite right. And heaven knows where they came from originally. And yet, there were already only a handful like him left when we met. They kept disappearing, Crossing over, I think they called it. Anyway, he was so amused by the look on my face as I dashed past, that he carved the scene on the rocks, as you know."

"But how did that help?" Christopher asked.

"Well, our next time-door took us to the other end of the time range, six thousand years from now, and we started looking for clues. I went back to the area where I'd met the old man, and lo and behold, there was your falcon's head. So I had the carving analyzed, and we were able to figure out within a hundred years when you were. Actually, we came back to about a hundred years from now, and heard the legends about the events you've just been through. That was enough to know the exact date the battle would commence."

His father sat back in the overstuffed chair. "You confounded us though, by entering the castle not with the army, but by some other means. How the devil did you get in there with all those ogres without being crushed?"

Christopher explained how he came to be there.

"He gets to have all the fun!" complained his brother from the sleeping loft above their heads.

"Next time it's your turn to battle ogres, dear." his mother said.

"Yeah, right." Alex replied.

Now Christopher told them of the dwarves' expectations about the boy 'from another world.'

His father and mother looked at each other. "That's why the Old Man of the Forest told us that it was important not to save him too soon." said his father. "He knew, even then, thousands of years before the event that things would come to this."

"I never did like his brother, that Sorcerer fellow." said Christopher's mother. "He had an attitude, if you ask me." From the rafters overhead, Heart 'whoooed' as if in agreement.

"Yeah, well, he sure had one when I talked to him." Christopher agreed.

"But what will happen now? Can we stay here, with them knowing?" Christopher's mother asked.

"Oh, I think our secret is safe with those in the know, but the less we are around to remind people, the better. As it is, I almost lost my time-travel license when I used the time-portal at the battle of the courtyard." Christopher's father replied.

"That's right! How could you do that?" asked Christopher. "You didn't really travel in time."

"Simple, actually. I just set it for 20 feet away as the where, and right now as the when." His father explained.

"But," he added, "if it wasn't for the positive aspects that came out of this, I think we'd have been in hot water. The Orange and Purple clans back together, the dwarves back in their castle and accepted by the men that populate the surrounding lands, and even the wolves are respected now."

"Of course, learning about The Old Man of the Forest and the Sorcerer didn't hurt either." added Christopher's mother. "The authorities are real curious to learn more about them. Imagine, an ancient race existed almost under our noses and we knew absolutely nothing about them."

"Yes, you got lucky, young man." she continued. "But next time you want a week of peace and quiet, I think maybe we'll just go fishing."

ABOUT THE AUTHOR

Rick Arbour spends his evenings in the hills of Western Massachusetts wondering just what sort of trouble will come Christopher's way in the future. He is assisted in his thoughts by three dogs, who probably know more than they will admit to.

24437128R00055

Made in the USA
Charleston, SC
22 November 2013